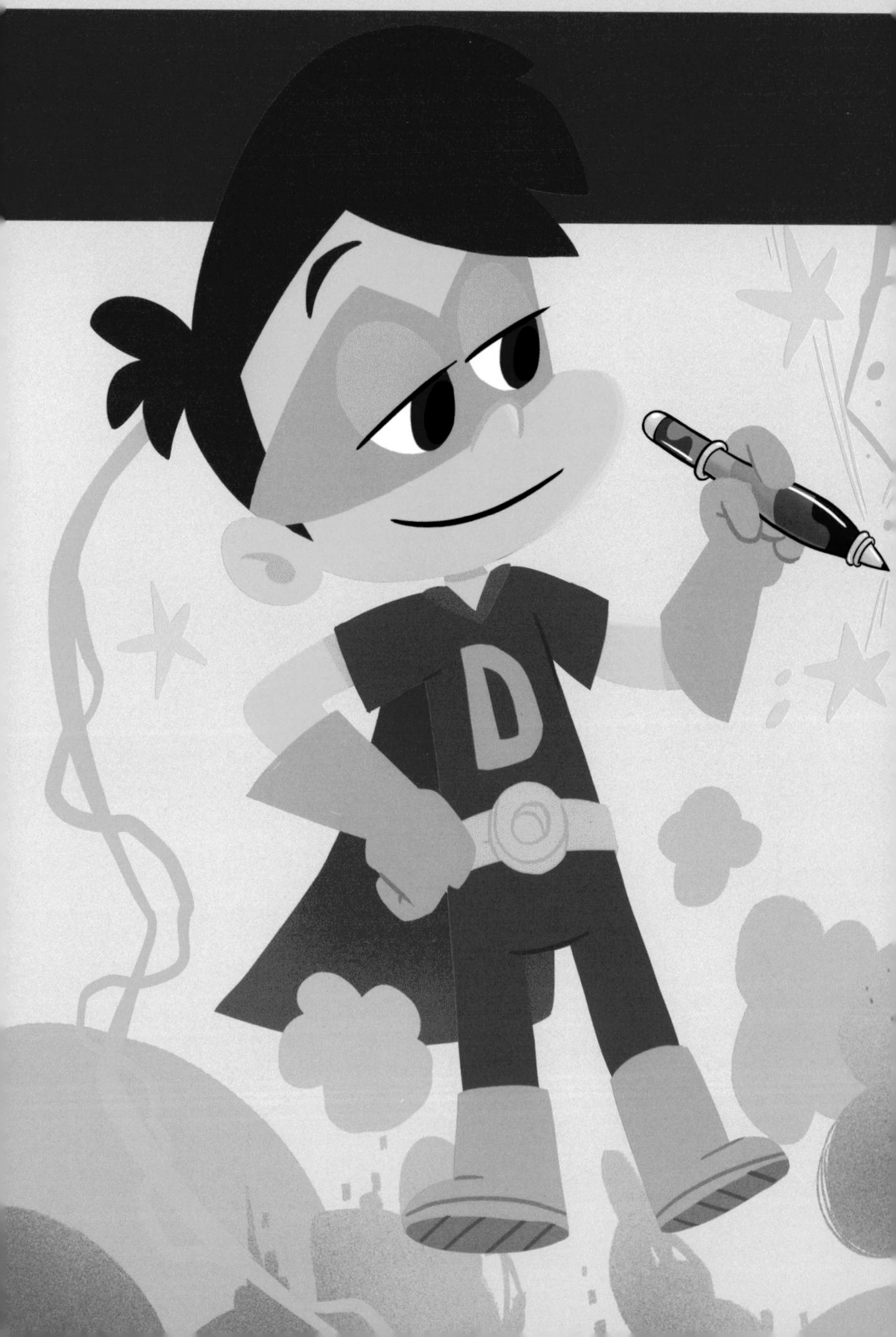

DREW PENDOUS

Versus Ray Blank #3

adapted by
David Lewman
based on the screenplay
by **Rachel O. Crouse**

illustrated by
Robert Dress
art direction by
Dan Markowitz

based on the series
COOL SCHOOL
and characters created by
Rob Kurtz

STERLING CHILDREN'S BOOKS
New York

STERLING CHILDREN'S BOOKS
New York

An Imprint of Sterling Publishing Co., Inc.
1166 Avenue of the Americas
New York, NY 10036

ISBN 978-1-4549-3110-2

Distributed in Canada by Sterling Publishing Co., Inc.
c/o Canadian Manda Group, 664 Annette Street
Toronto, Ontario M6S 2C8, Canada
Distributed in the United Kingdom by GMC Distribution Services
Castle Place, 166 High Street, Lewes, East Sussex BN7 1XU, England
Distributed in Australia by NewSouth Books
University of New South Wales, Sydney, NSW 2052, Australia

For information about custom editions, special sales, and premium and corporate purchases, please contact Sterling Special Sales at 800-805-5489 or specialsales@sterlingpublishing.com.

Manufactured in China

Lot #:
2 4 6 8 10 9 7 5 3 1
06/19

sterlingpublishing.com

CONTENTS

YES, it's time for another **amazing adventure** starring everyone's favorite superhero . . .

THE STUPENDOUS DREW PENDOUS AND HIS MIGHTY PEN ULTIMATE!

HI, EVERYONE! YOU'VE MET THE SUPER-NOT-NICE, EXTRA-EVIL RAY BLANK, WHO ERASES EVERYTHING I DRAW, BUT DID YOU KNOW HOW RAY AND I FIRST MET? HERE'S THE TRUE STORY!

Drew and his friends were in the Cool School library. They loved going to the library, because they got to sit on the floor and listen to Ms. Booksy read stories. She was a very good reader. She even did funny voices for all the different characters in the books.

"Good morning, students!" Ms. Booksy said cheerfully.

"Good morning, Ms. Booksy!" they answered.

"I have a special surprise for you," she said.

The kids looked at one another and grinned. They liked the sound of a special surprise!

"Today I am **NOT** going to read you a story," Ms. Booksy said.

The kids stopped grinning. **NOT** read a story?! How was **THAT** a special surprise? It sounded more like a punishment!

"Instead, we're going to make up our **OWN** story!" Ms. Booksy explained. "And we're going to do it together!"

The kids started to smile again. Making up a story sounded like fun!

Ms. Booksy said that she would start the story. Then she'd point at one of the students. That person would tell the next part of the story. When Ms. Booksy pointed at someone else, the new storyteller would take over where the last person left off.

9

"Understand?" Ms. Booksy asked. "Crystal **clear?** Or clear as **mud?"**

"Crystal clear!" the kids shouted.

"All right!" Ms. Booksy said. "Then let's start our totally new, **made-up story!**

ONCE UPON A TIME, THERE WAS A . . .
. . . PIRATE!
THIS PIRATE LOVED SAILING AROUND THE WORLD IN HIS . . .
ME? OKAY, UM, IN HIS . . .

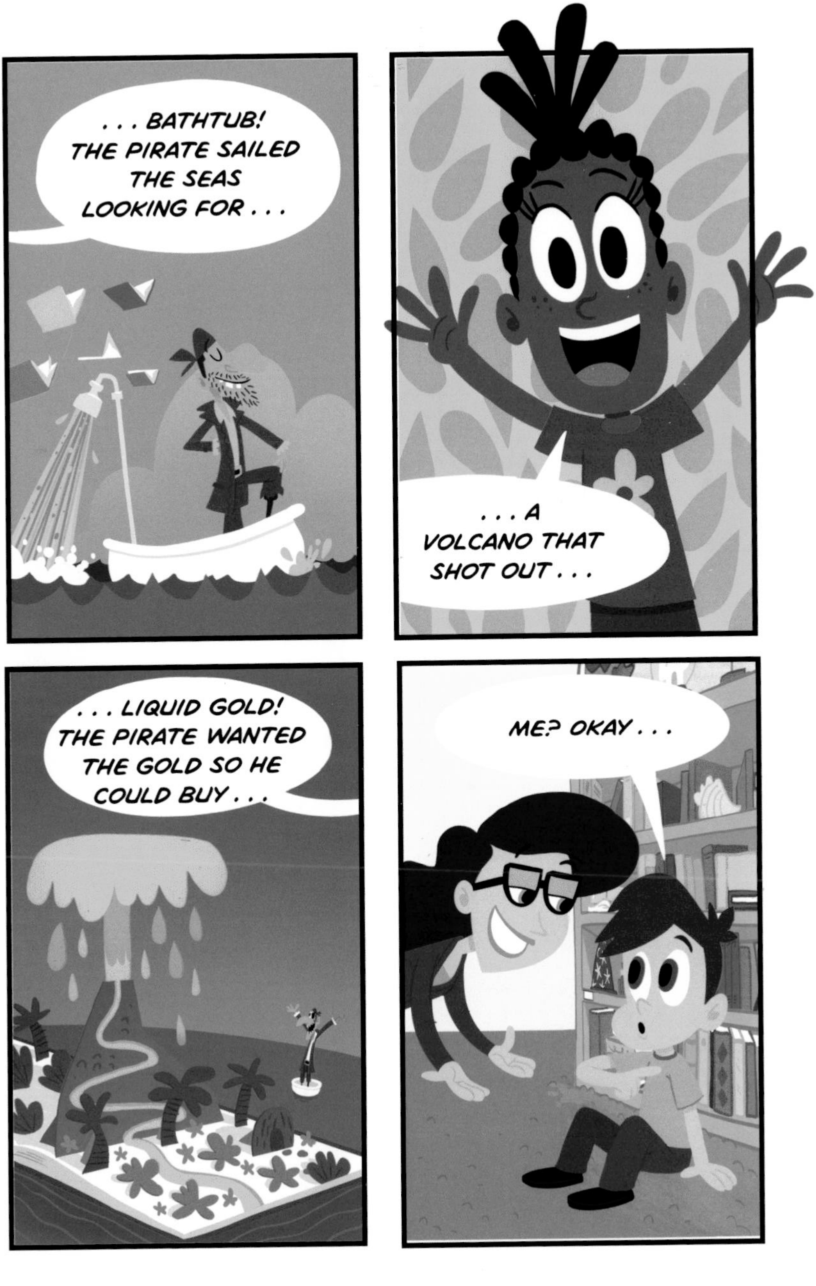
. . . BATHTUB! THE PIRATE SAILED THE SEAS LOOKING FOR . . .
. . . A VOLCANO THAT SHOT OUT . . .
. . . LIQUID GOLD! THE PIRATE WANTED THE GOLD SO HE COULD BUY . . .
ME? OKAY . . .

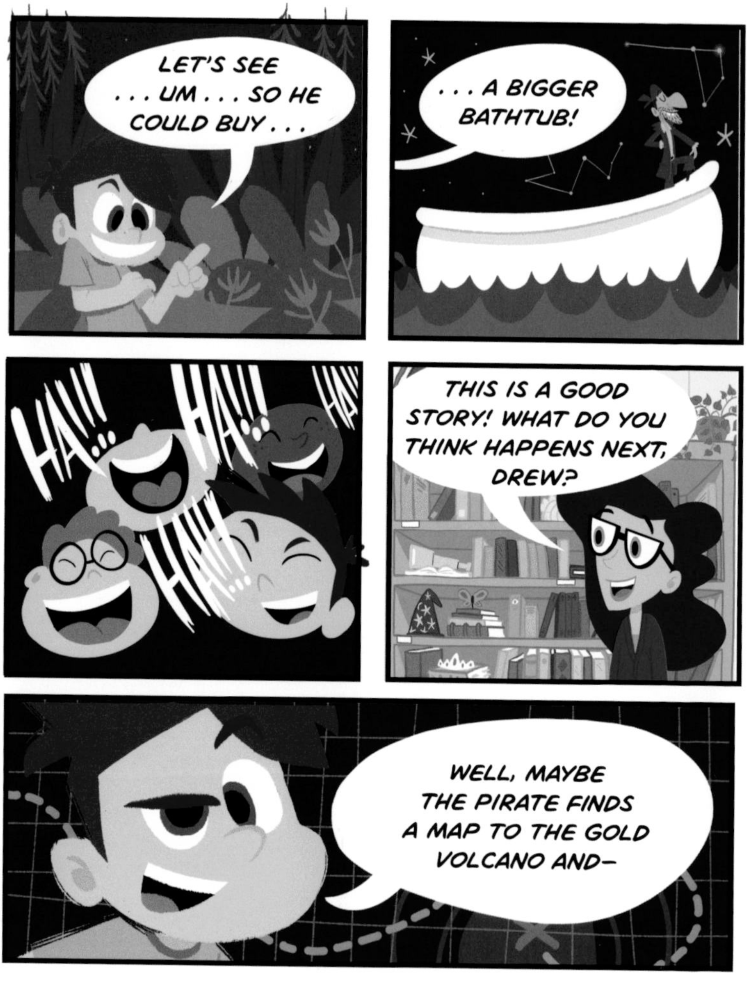
LET'S SEE . . . UM . . . SO HE COULD BUY . . .
. . . A BIGGER BATHTUB!
HA!!
HA!!
HA!!
HA!
THIS IS A GOOD STORY! WHAT DO YOU THINK HAPPENS NEXT, DREW?
WELL, MAYBE THE PIRATE FINDS A MAP TO THE GOLD VOLCANO AND—

But before Drew could finish his idea, Akiko burst into the library. "There you are, Drew Pendous!" he cried, pointing his finger accusingly. "Why did you do it? WHY?!"

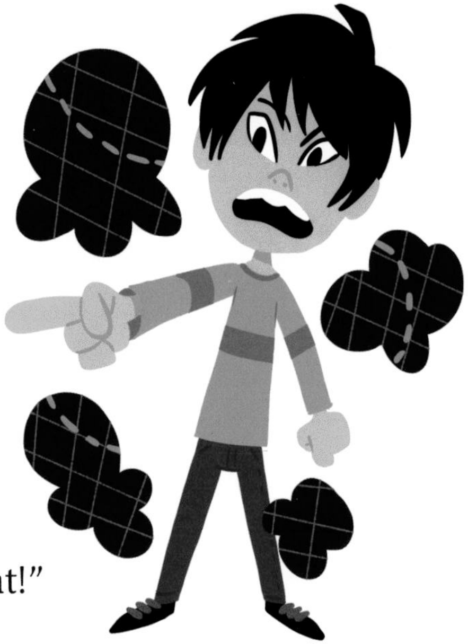

"Do ***what?"***

Drew asked, puzzled.

"Erase my homework!"

Akiko said.

"I didn't erase your homework!" Drew said. "I would ***never*** do that!"

Akiko didn't look convinced by Drew's denial. "All I know is that my project is ***gone,*** and I saw you leaving the classroom. At least, I saw the back of you. And you were ***wearing a cape!*** You're the only kid in Cool School who goes around wearing a cape some of the time."

Everyone stared at Drew. They'd all seen him wearing his superhero cape. Could Akiko be right? Could Drew have erased Akiko's homework?

CHAPTER TWO

DREW FELT everyone's eyes on him. "You didn't ***see me!"*** he protested. "You must have seen ***someone else!"***

"Oh, yeah?" Akiko said. "Prove it, homework-eraser!"

Drew thought for a second. Then he smiled. "Wait, you said you saw me coming out of the classroom, right?"

"Right!" Akiko said. "Where I'd left my homework! That ***you erased!"***

Drew shook his head. "You couldn't have seen me coming out of the classroom this morning, because I've been ***right here*** in the library ***the whole time!"***

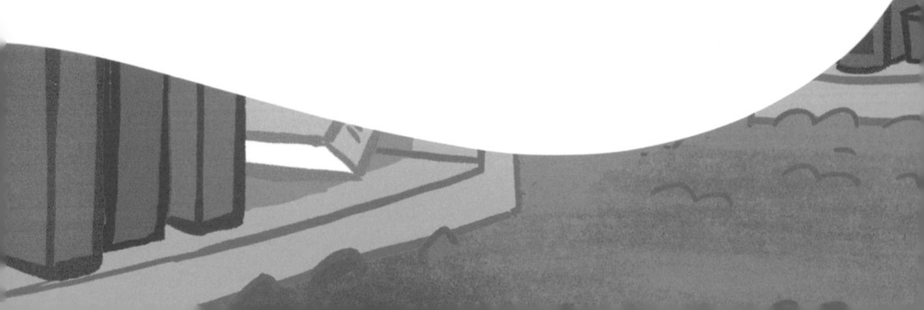

Ms. Booksy and the other kids nodded. ***Drew was right***. They'd all seen him sitting in the library with them. He'd been in the library all morning. Akiko must have seen ***someone else***.

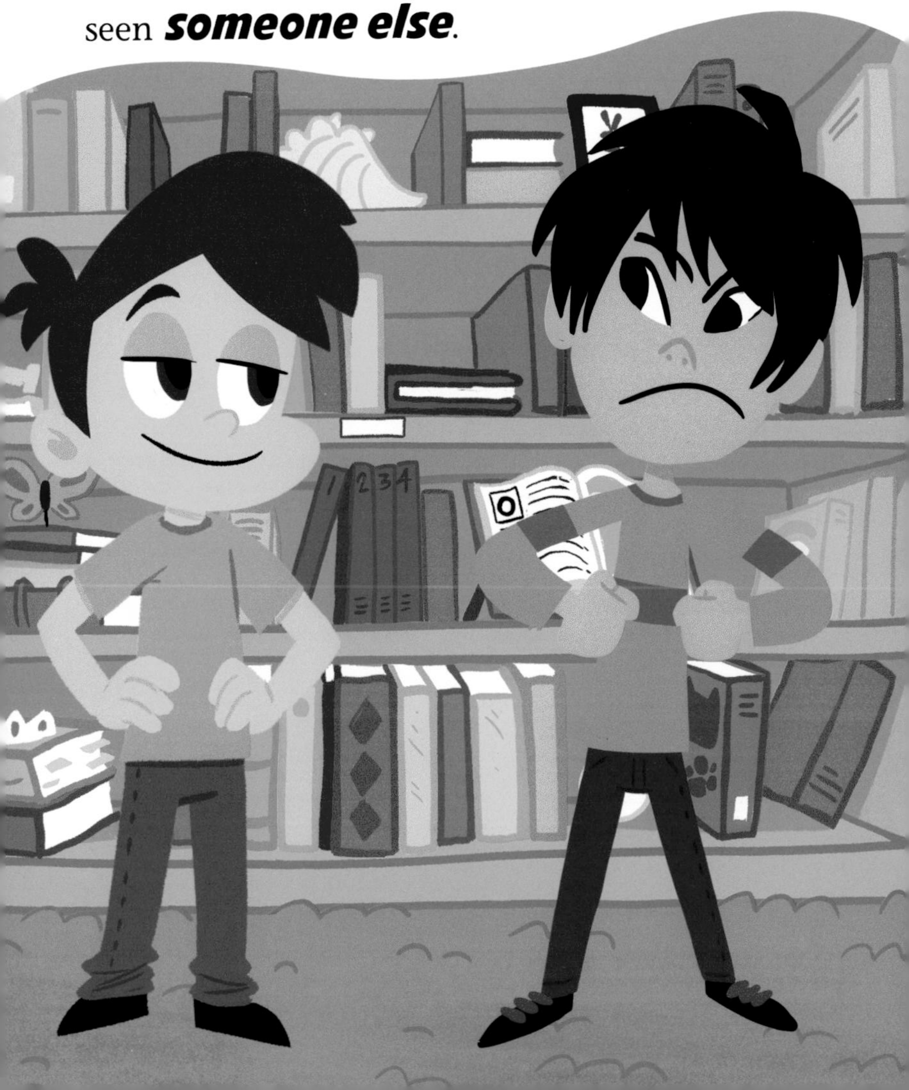

Later that morning, Drew, Nikki, and Robby were walking down the halls of Cool School. They kept hearing kids complaining about stuff that had gone missing.

"Somebody took my headphones!" one boy wailed.

"Well, **somebody took my backpack!"** a girl snapped.

"Somebody took MY SHOES!" shouted a boy walking down the hallway in his socks.

Even worse, kids were saying that they'd seen ***the thief running*** through Cool School ***wearing a cape!*** And that he looked a lot ***like Drew!***

"It wasn't me!" Drew kept telling all the other students. "I would never do that! ***I'm not a thief!"***

The lunch bell rang! Which could mean only one thing: ***LUNCH TIME!***

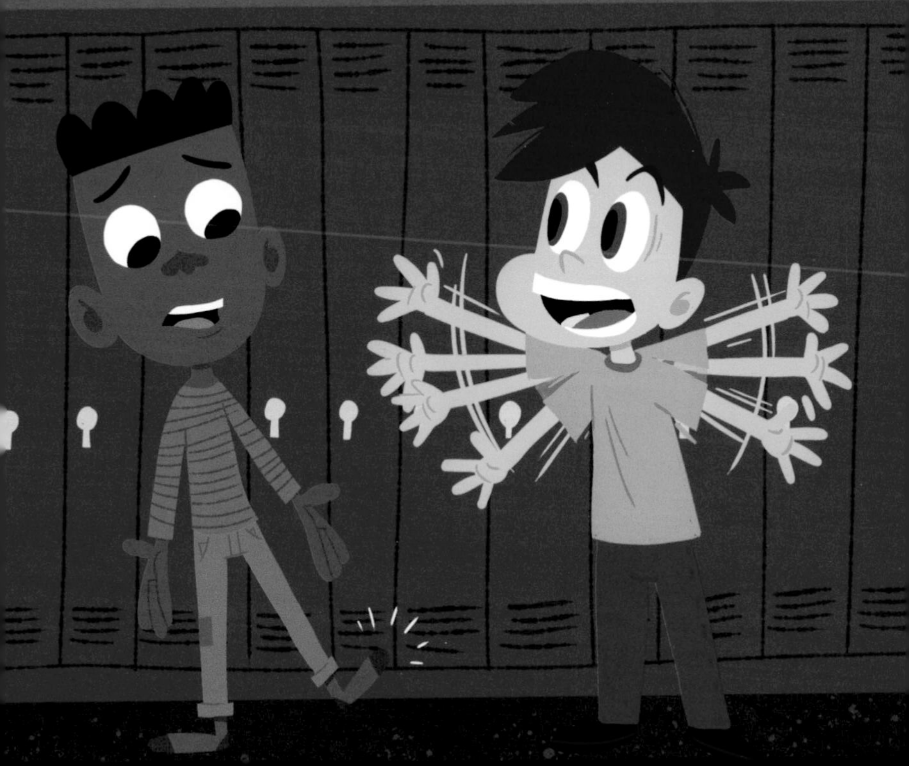

As Drew and his friends hurried in to eat, they passed kids running out of the cafeteria looking sick.

"Eww!" one girl said.

"Yuck!" a boy said.

"Gross!" another boy groaned, holding his stomach.

Inside the cafeteria, Drew saw that someone had messed with the menu sign. ***Instead of pizza day*** and

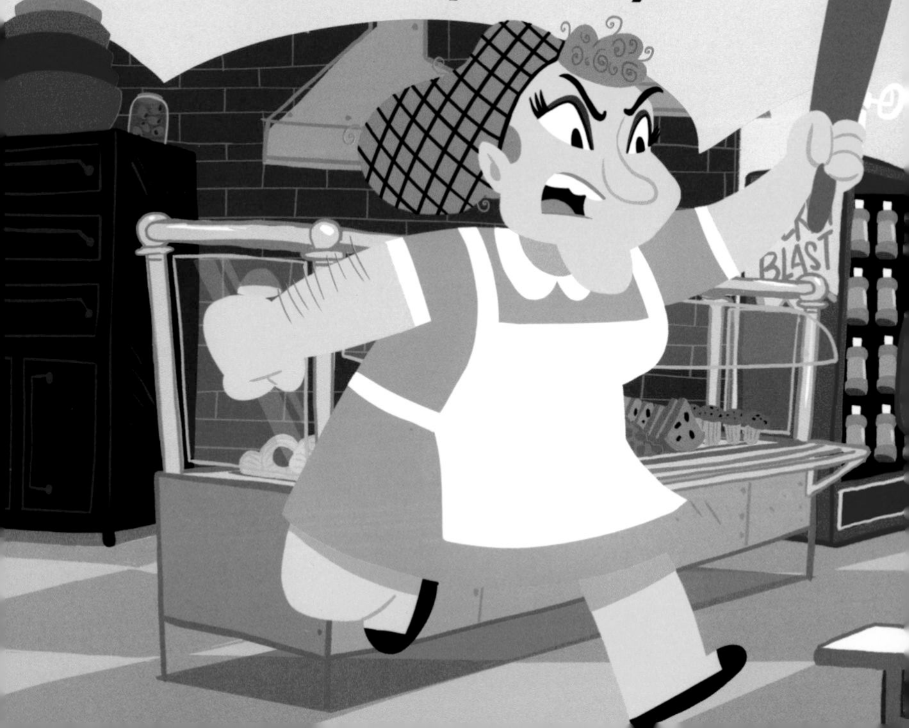
BLAST

spaghetti, it read ***sloppy joes with grape jelly and onion slices and cauliflower tacos with liver!***

The lunch lady had accidentally ***SERVED*** those gross dishes. ***BLECH!***

"But this is supposed to be pizza day!" Drew cried. "This is getting ***really bad."***

The ***lunch lady*** came out of the kitchen angrily waving her rolling pin.

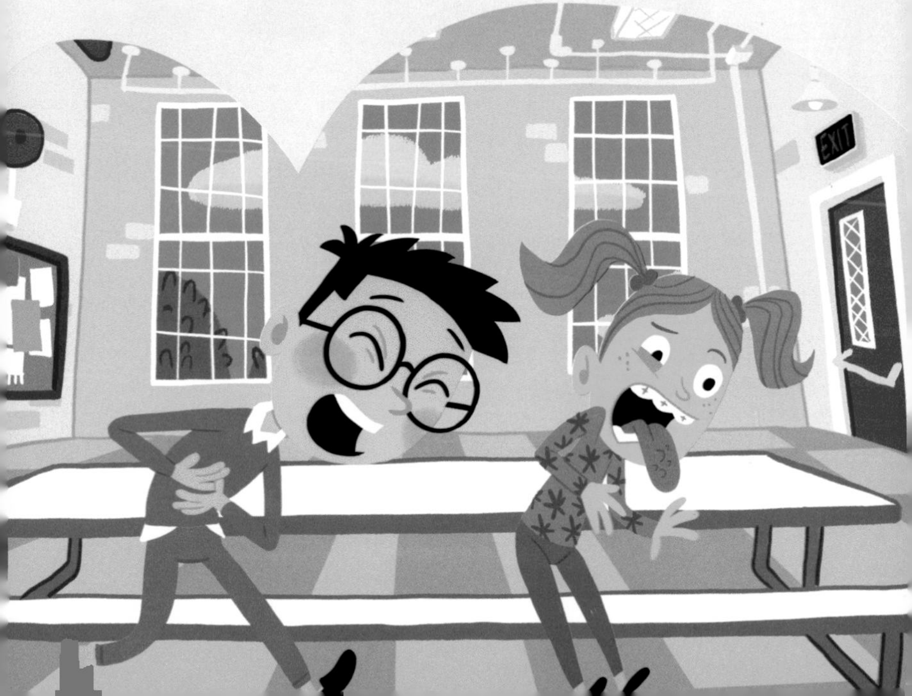
EXIT

"There he is!" she yelled in her raspy voice. ***"That's who did it!"*** She pointed her rolling pin right at Drew!

"No way!" Drew insisted. "I would ***NEVER*** mess with pizza day."

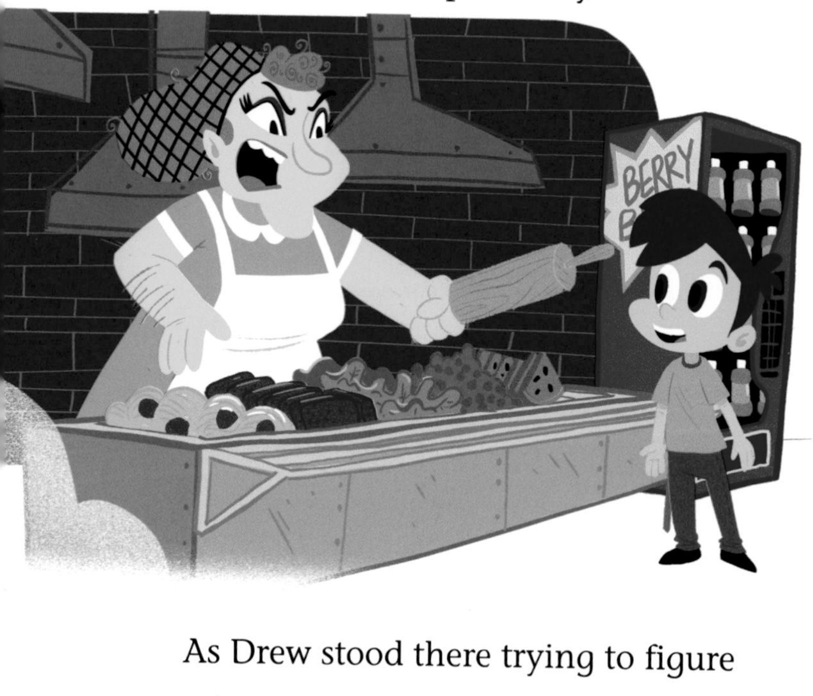
BERRY

As Drew stood there trying to figure out what he was going to eat for lunch, ***Crafty Carol*** burst through the cafeteria doors. "Oh, ***THERE*** you are!" she called out when she spotted Drew.

"Hi, Crafty Carol. Is something wrong??" Drew asked, confused. Why did Crafty Carol look so annoyed with him?

She stomped right up to him. ***"Drew, did you erase a bunch of my crafting supplies?*** I was about to use them to craft something new with my students: a macaroni castle!"

Drew's stomach growled. Macaroni sounded good. ***"No way!*** I love macaroni!" he said. ***"I promise."***

Everyone in the cafeteria was staring at Drew like he was a horrible, guilty bad guy. ***"I didn't do*** any of these ***bad things,"*** he announced. "But if you just give me a little time, I'll figure out who did!"

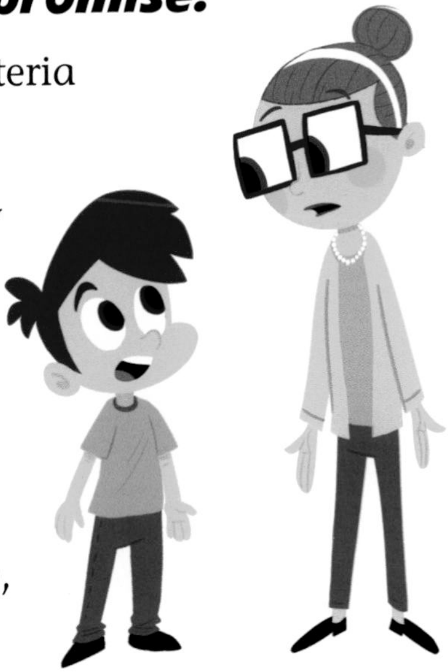

CHAPTER THREE

AS SOON AS DREW

left the cafeteria, he knew he had to act fast, so he used his **Pen Ultimate** to draw a big *D* on his chest and turn into his superhero self. Then he looked around for anything that might have gone ***missing***. It didn't take him long to spot a blank sign in the hallway. *I remember that sign*, he thought to himself. *It used to say* NO RUNNING! *But the words are gone.* It was as though someone had ***erased*** all the other words on the sign.

Drew spotted a book lying on the hallway floor near the sign. He picked it up and saw that its words had been erased too! *Who is erasing all these words?* he wondered.

Farther down the hallway, **another book** lay on the floor. Drew ran over and picked it up. More **missing** words! He saw more books on the floor and followed the trail to see where it led. He went down the hallway, through the doors, and out onto the Cool School playground.

Drew looked around. ***Everything*** looked normal. It was a sunny day, and kids were playing on the equipment.

But then something really weird happened: A boy was swinging on the swings when, all of a sudden, the swings disappeared! ***"WHOA!"*** the kid yelled as he flew through the air, landing on his feet. ***"Hey!*** Where'd the swings go?"

Another kid was climbing on the monkey bars. But all of a sudden, the monkey bars ***disappeared!*** The kid

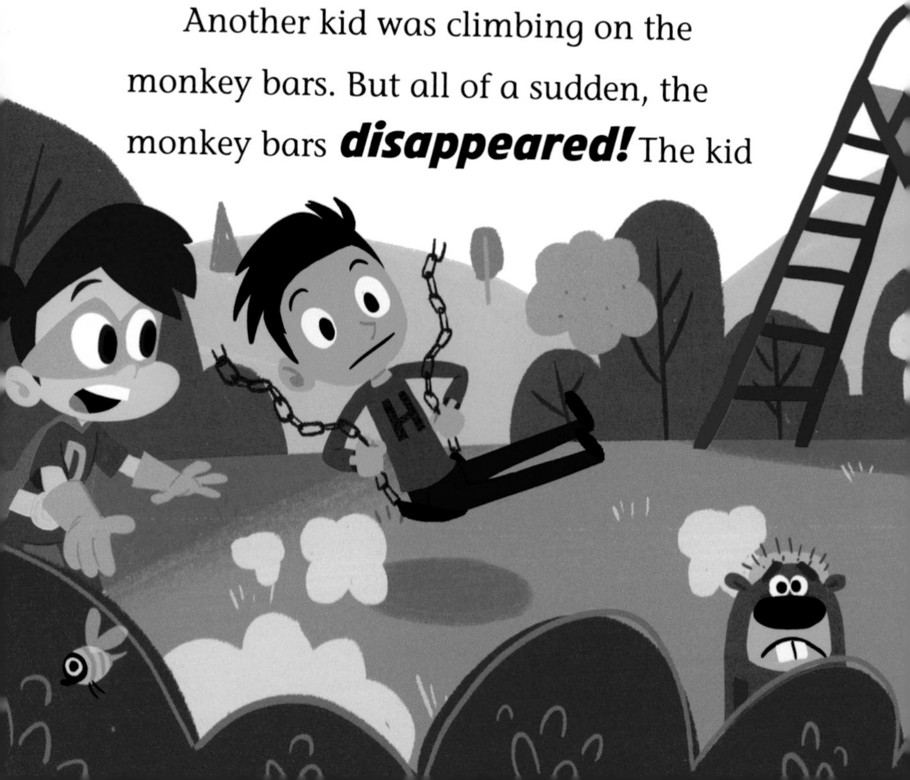

tumbled to the sand. She wasn't hurt, but she was very confused. She just sat there in the sand, saying, "Where'd the monkey bars go?"

A boy slid down the slide, saying, **"Wheee!"** When he reached the bottom, he turned around, ready to climb the ladder and slide down again. But the slide had disappeared! **"Huh?!"** he said, staring at the spot where the slide used to be.

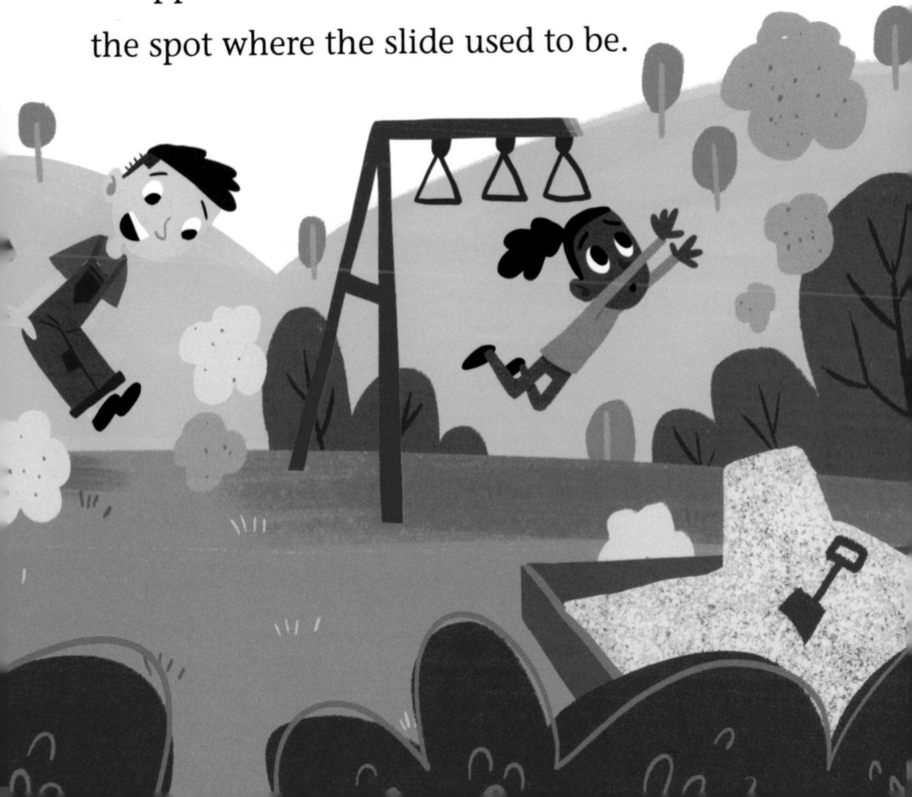

Drew saw the playground equipment disappear. And he saw something else: a mysterious figure ran by ***wearing a cape***. "That guy looks like me!" Drew exclaimed. "It's like I have . . ."

". . . AN EVIL TWIN!" said a raspy voice behind him.

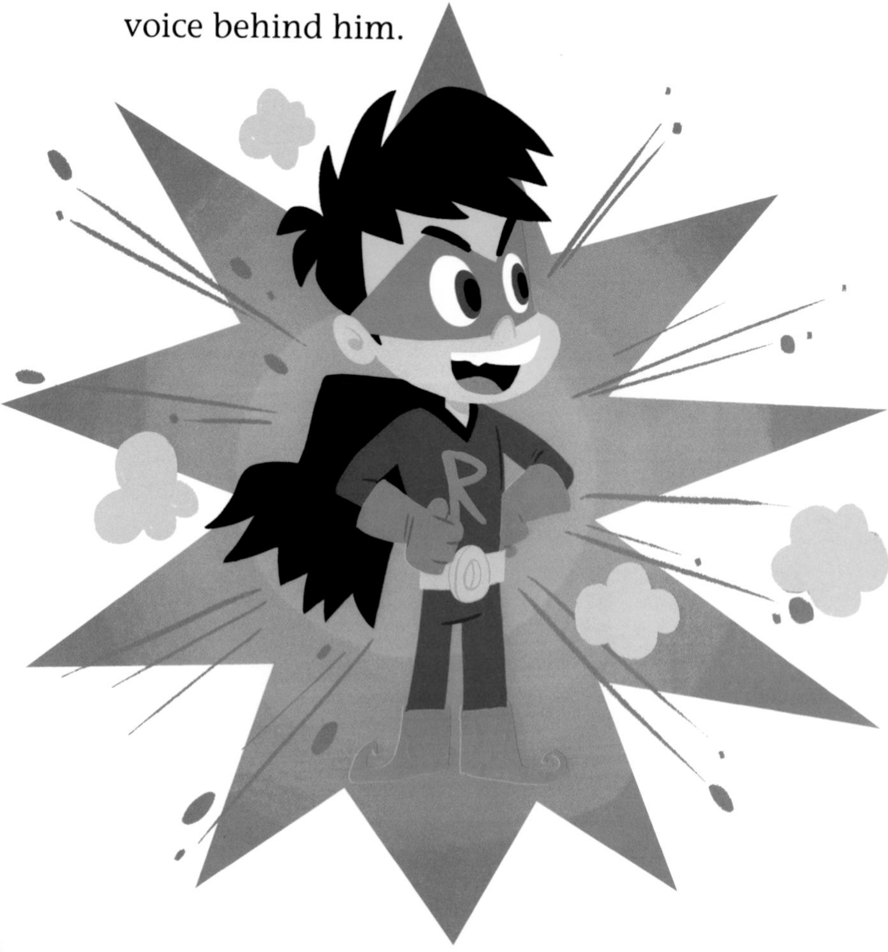

R

Drew whipped around and saw ***a boy*** just his size. He looked a lot like Drew, but he had black hair, black eyebrows, and blue eyes. He was wearing purple pants, a purple shirt with a green on it, a gold belt, green boots, green gloves, a green mask, and ***a black cape!***

Who ***WAS*** this mysterious ***evil twin?!***

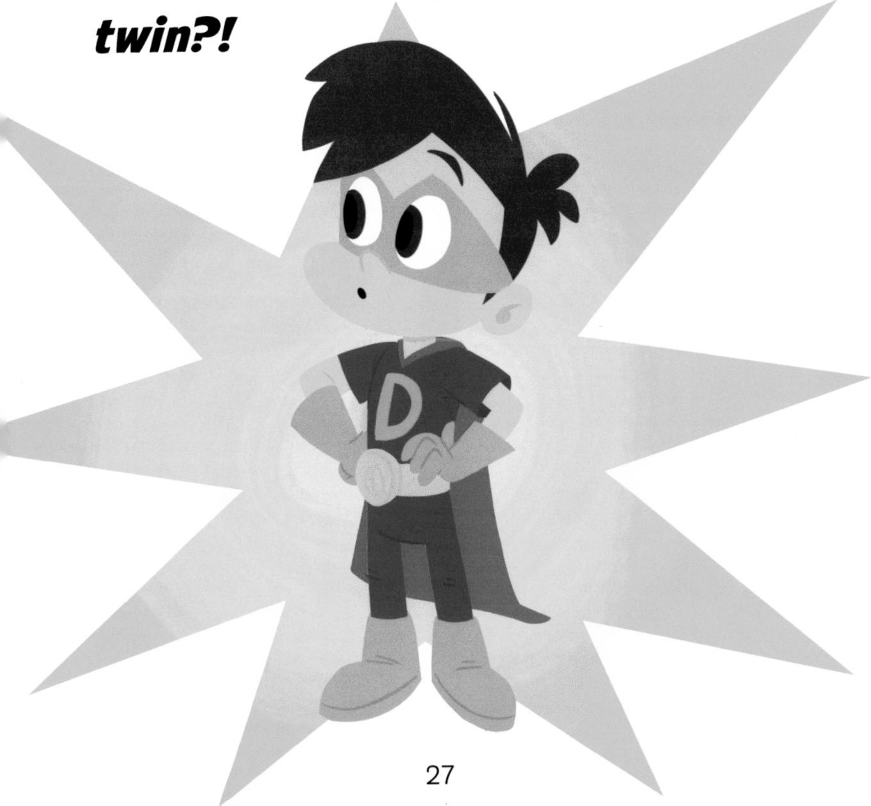

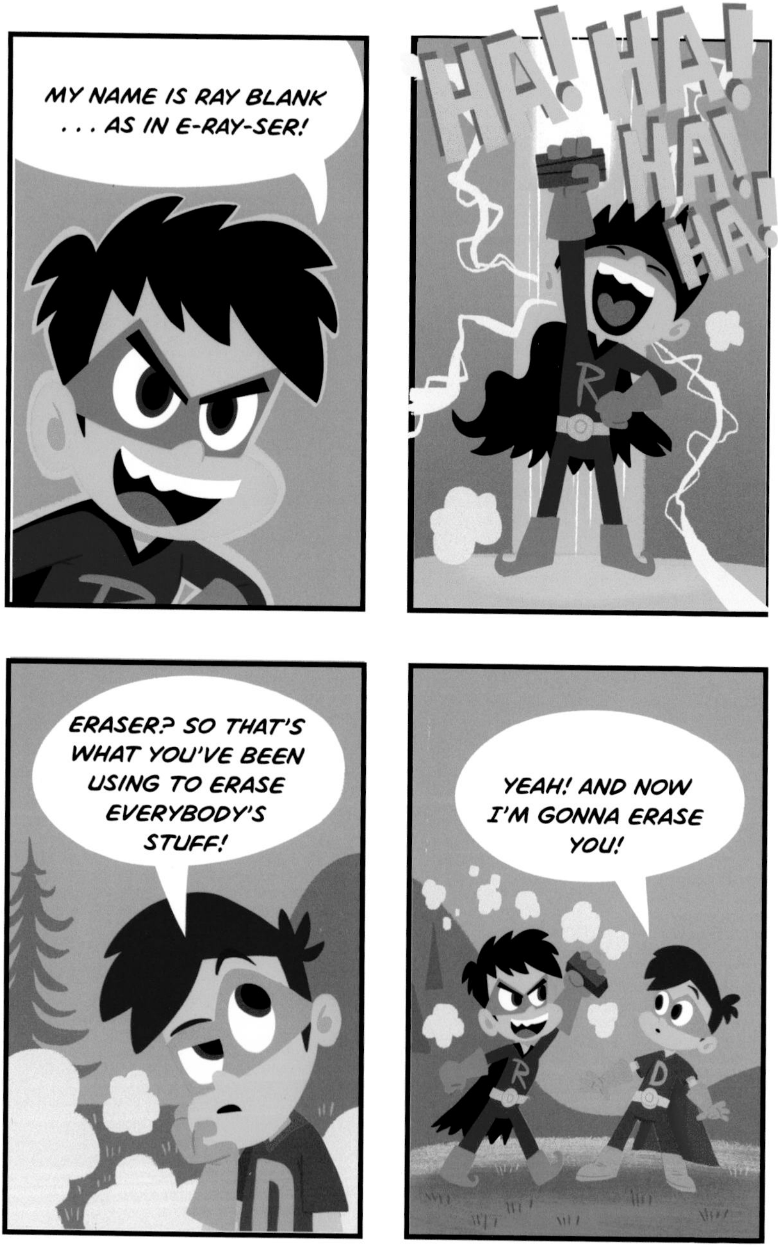
MY NAME IS RAY BLANK . . . AS IN E-RAY-SER!
HA! HA! HA! HA!
ERASER? SO THAT'S WHAT YOU'VE BEEN USING TO ERASE EVERYBODY'S STUFF!
YEAH! AND NOW I'M GONNA ERASE YOU!

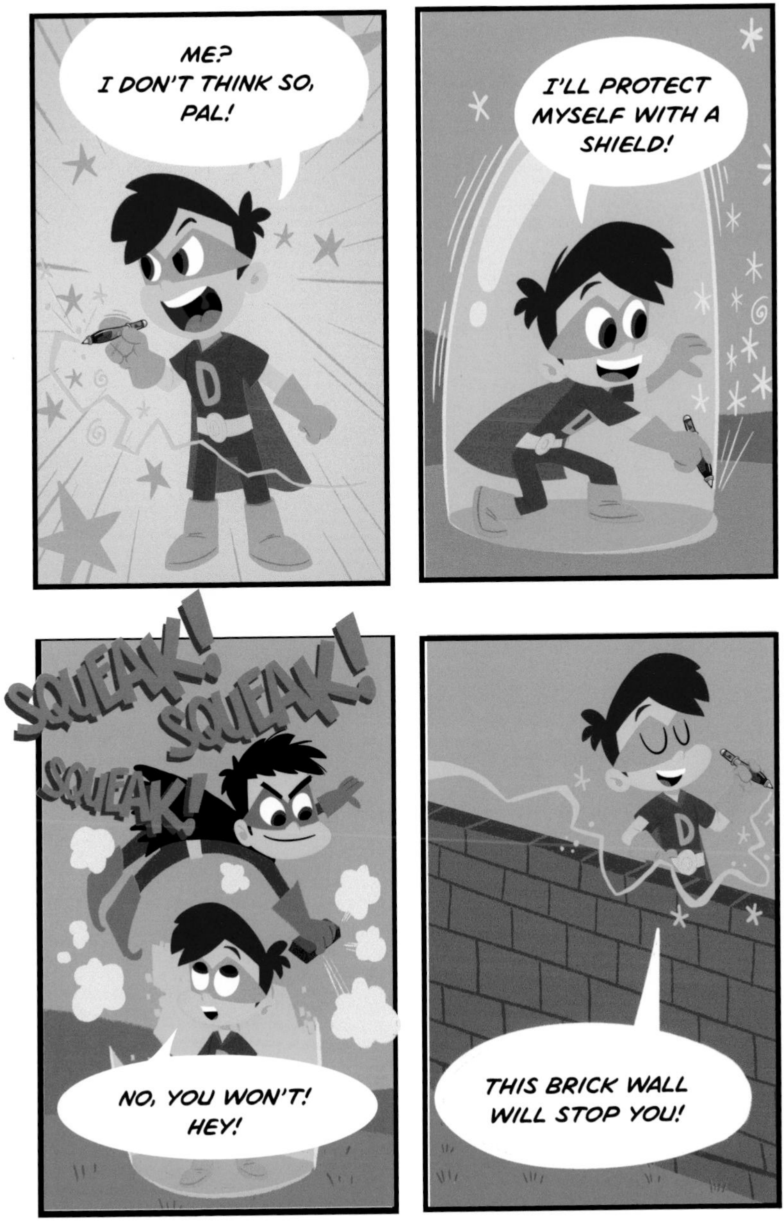
ME? I DON'T THINK SO, PAL!
I'LL PROTECT MYSELF WITH A SHIELD!
SQUEAK! SQUEAK! SQUEAK!
NO, YOU WON'T! HEY!
THIS BRICK WALL WILL STOP YOU!

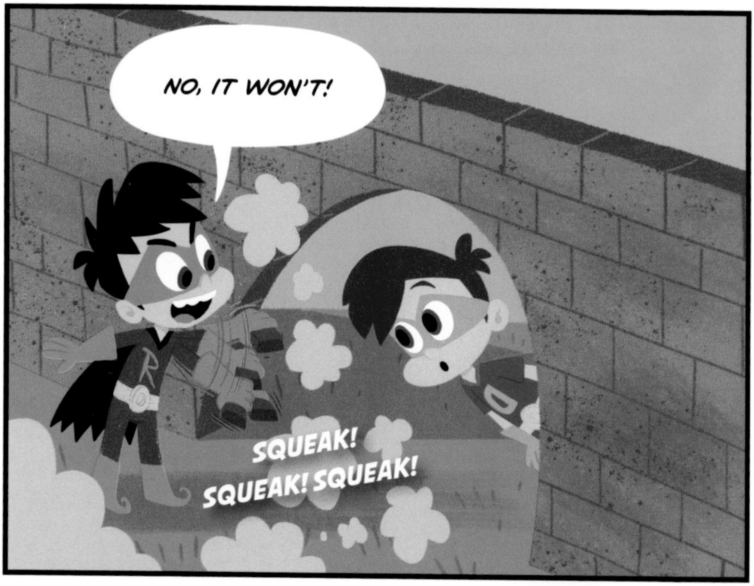
NO, IT WON'T!
SQUEAK! SQUEAK! SQUEAK!

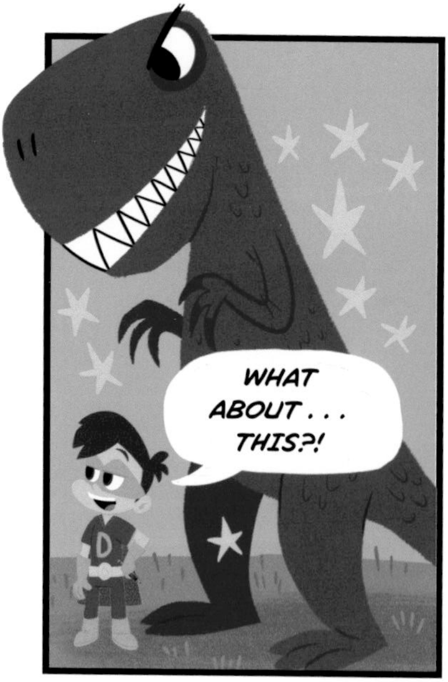
WHAT ABOUT . . . THIS?!

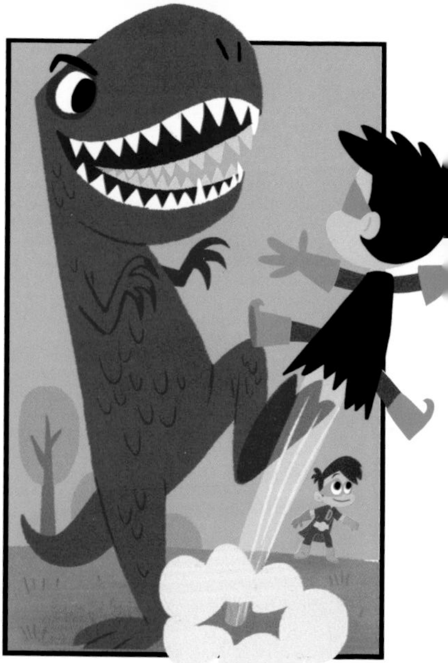

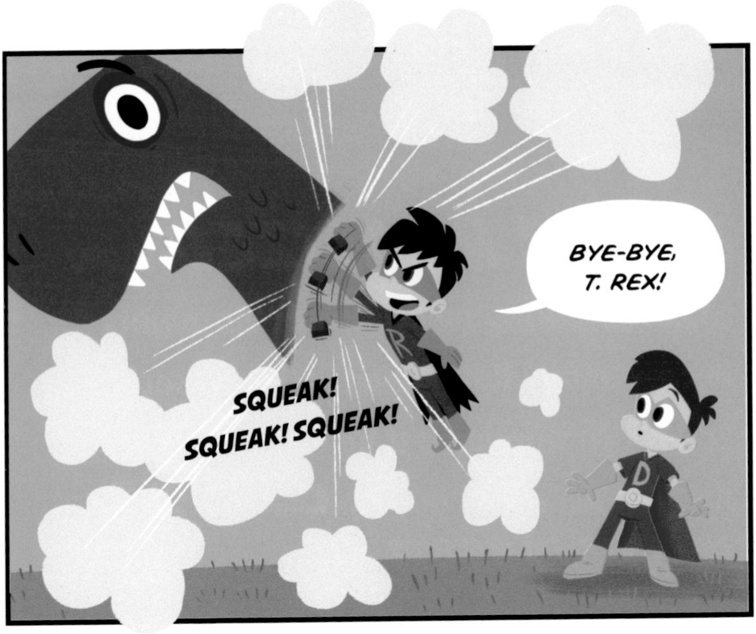
BYE-BYE, T. REX!
SQUEAK! SQUEAK! SQUEAK!

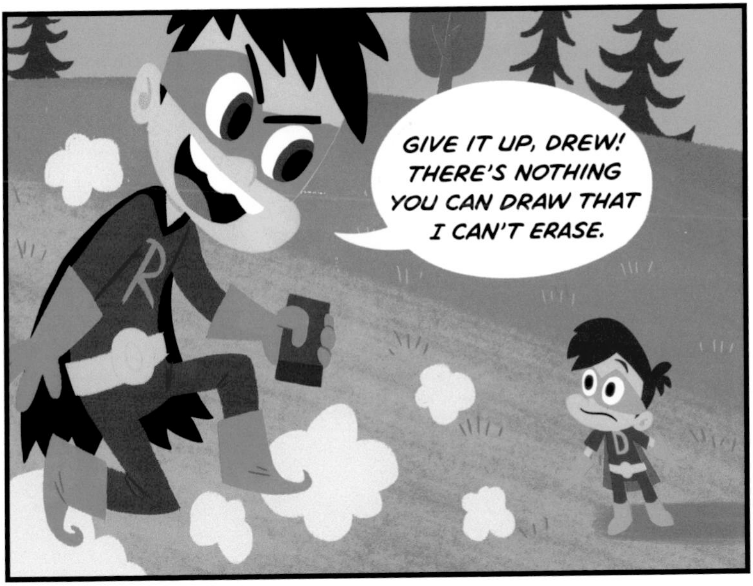
GIVE IT UP, DREW! THERE'S NOTHING YOU CAN DRAW THAT I CAN'T ERASE.

CHAPTER FOUR

DREW REALIZED it was true! Everything he drew with his mighty Pen Ultimate, Ray erased with his Magic Eraser! He wondered if he had finally met his match—a bad guy he **COULDN'T POSSIBLY BEAT!**

"Okay, Ray," Drew said. "You've proven you can erase anything I draw."

"That's right, Drew," Ray said, grinning an evil grin and nodding. **"Anything!"**

"But why?" Drew asked his evil twin.

"Why are you going around erasing all this stuff? What do you want?"

Ray raised his fists above his head in a classic evil-villain pose. ***"What do I want?"*** he cried. "I'll tell you what I want! I want ***CHAOS! CRAZINESS! DESTRUCTION!"*** He laughed a long, loud, evil laugh.

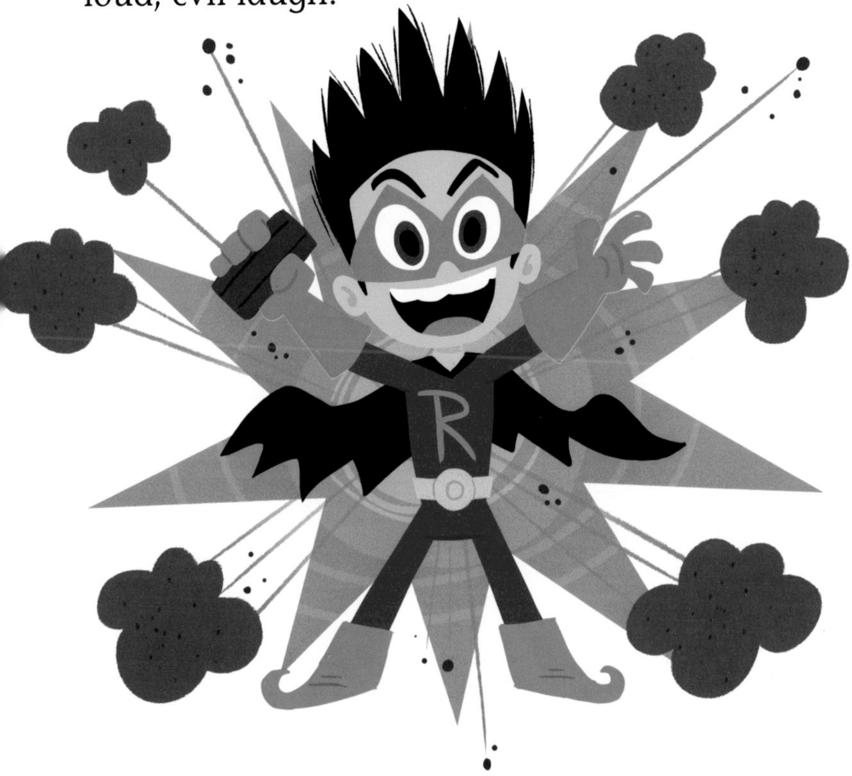
R

When Ray had finally finished laughing, Drew said, **_"I don't believe you."_**

"Huh?" Ray said, surprised. "What do you mean you don't believe me?"

Drew shrugged. "What you said sounds like something you read in a comic book or heard on TV. But I don't know why you would want those things. It's not very nice. What do you **_REALLY_** want?"

All of a sudden, Ray didn't look so evil. He looked down at the ground and drew squiggles in the playground dirt with the toe of his green boot. "Well," he said quietly, "if I tell you, you have to promise not to laugh."

Drew looked at Ray and smiled. "I promise."

Ray took a deep breath and let it out with a big sigh. **_"I just want to go to Cool School."_**

Now it was Drew's turn to look surprised. "What?!" he said. "You do?"

Ray nodded.

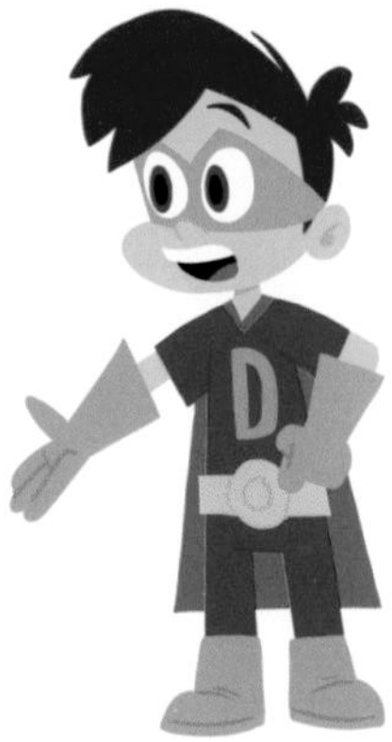

"Well, you sure picked a funny way to show it," Drew said, "erasing our signs and our books and our playground equipment. But I guess it makes sense that you want to go to ***Cool School***. It is the best school in the universe! What school do you go to now?"

Ray made a disgusted face. "Where I come from, there's only one place to go to school: ***Cruel School!***"

"Cruel School?" Drew said. "That doesn't sound like much fun."

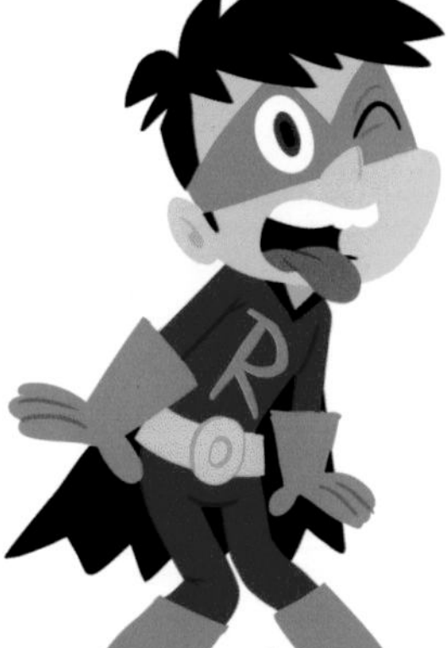

"It isn't," Ray agreed. ***"It's no fun at all. Cruel School is terrible!"***

"Oh, I bet it's not all THAT bad," Drew said.

"Oh yeah?" Ray said. "Come on. I'll **SHOW** you. Follow me."

Ray turned and ran away from the playground equipment, toward the far corner of the schoolyard. Drew ran after him. **"Wait!"** he called after Ray. **"Where are we going?"** He knew that there wasn't any place called **"Cruel School"** on the grounds of Cool School.

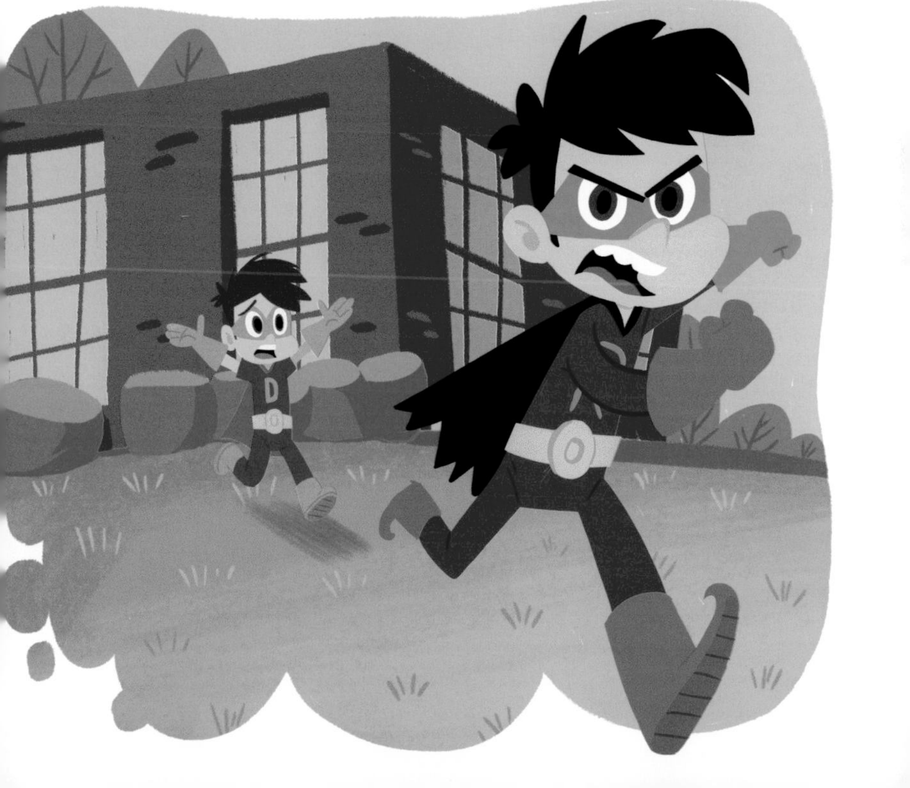
D

When he reached the farthest corner of the schoolyard, Ray stopped and waited for Drew to catch up. There was no playground equipment or basketball court or baseball diamond in this corner of the property. All Drew saw was a big, scraggly bush.

"Is that supposed to be **_Cruel School?_**" Drew asked. "That bush?"

Ray snorted. "Of course not. Cruel School isn't a bush; it's a school! A terrible, awful school!"

Drew looked confused. ***"Then what are we doing here?"***

"Just watch," Ray said.

He took out his ***Magic Eraser*** and started erasing the bush. When he was done, Drew saw a door in a frame. But there was nothing behind the door.

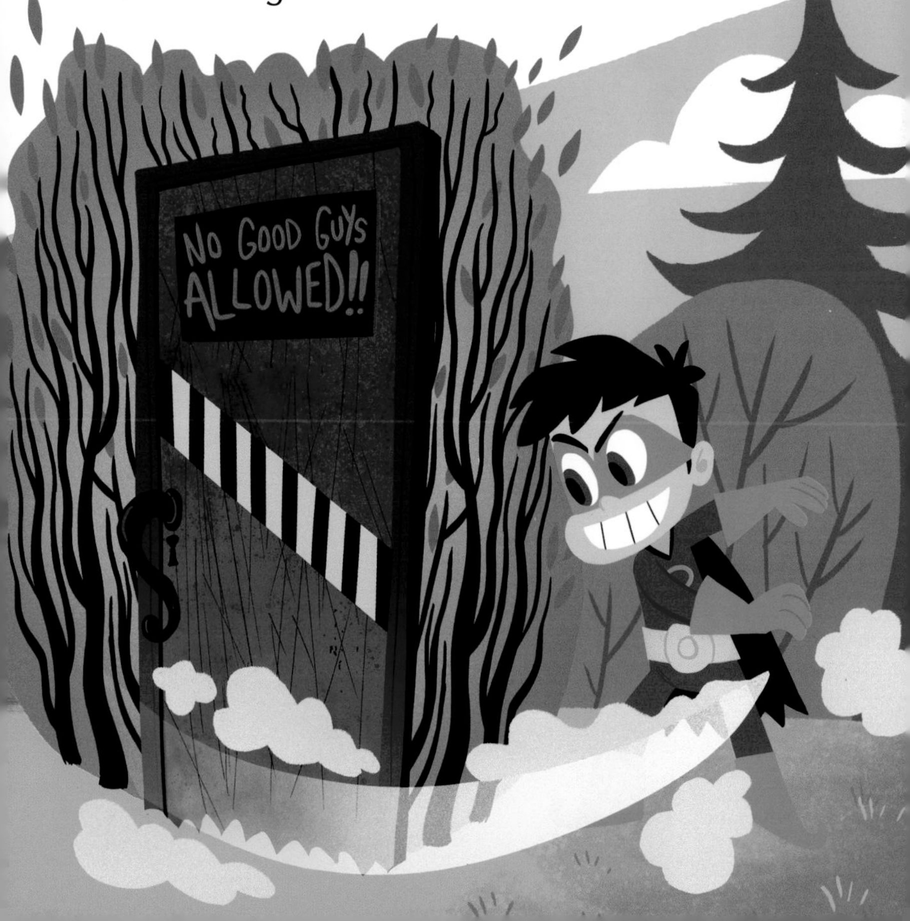
NO GOOD GUYS ALLOWED!!

"What's that?" Drew asked.

"This," Ray explained, "is the portal to Cruel School. It's what we're gonna use to get from your world to my world."

"How?" Drew asked.

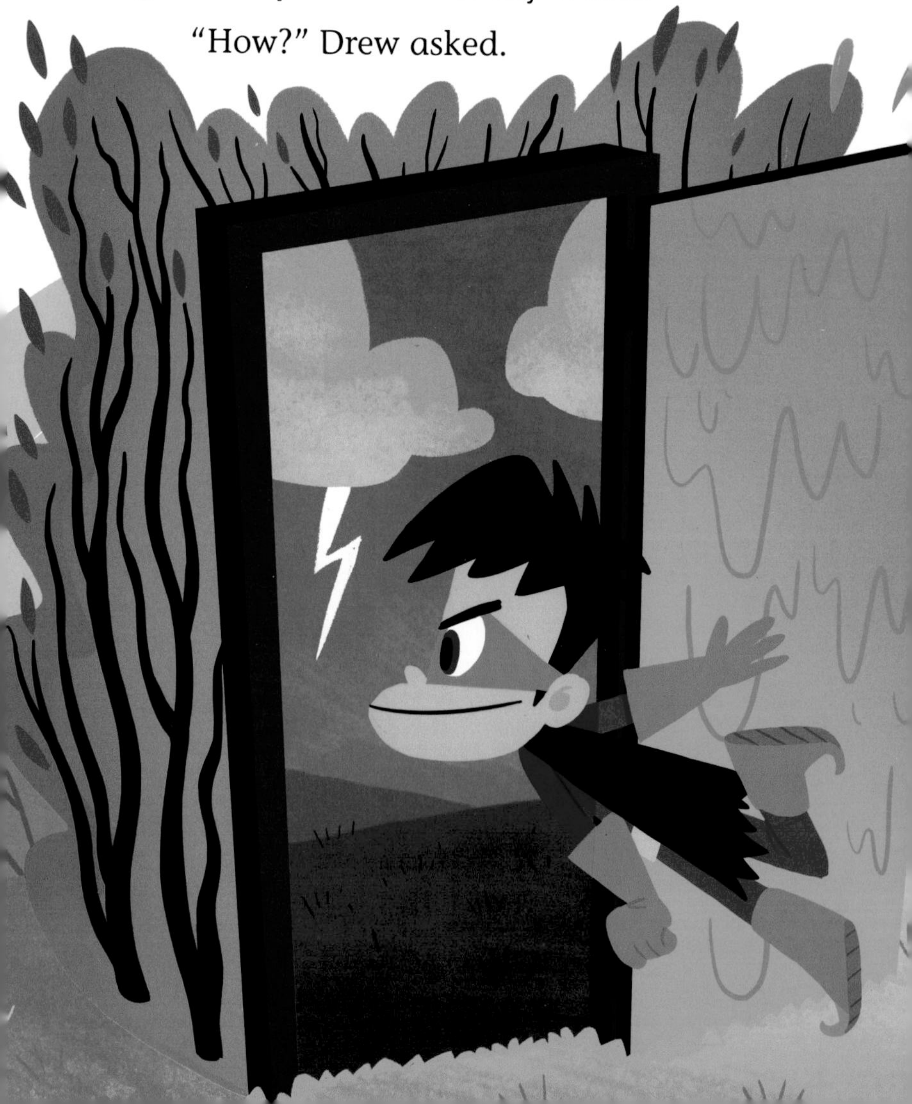

"Simple," Ray answered. "First we open the door." He grabbed the handle and swung the door open. On the other side, Drew got a glimpse of a dark, cloudy sky. "And then we jump through. Come on!"

Ray jumped through the open portal into the gloomy, stormy world. Drew took a big breath and jumped through after him.

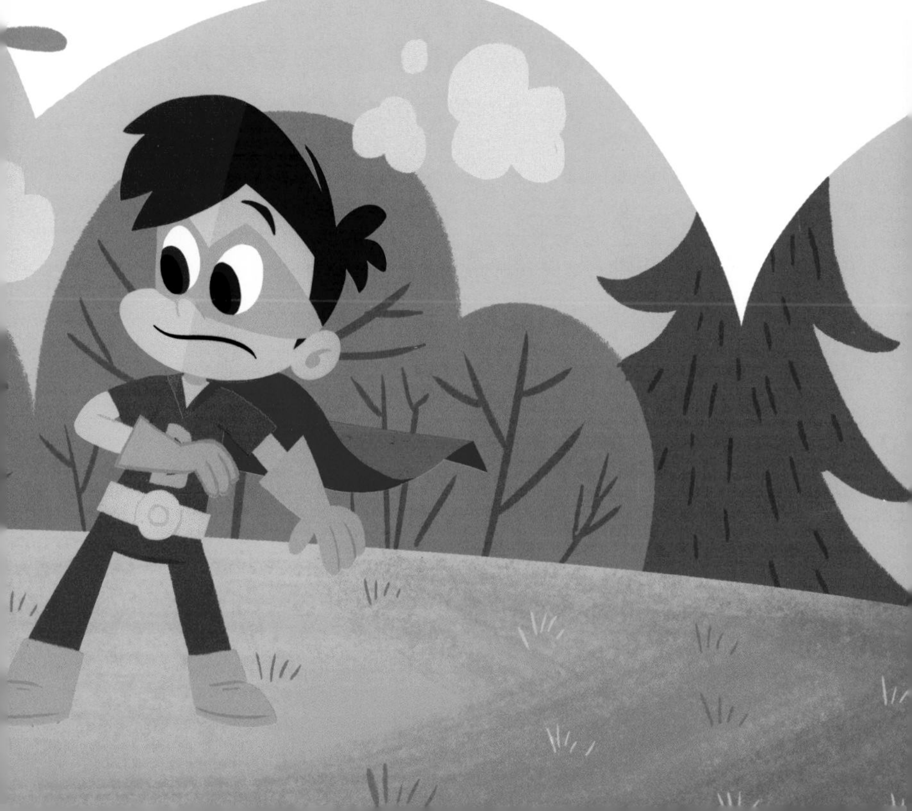

CHAPTER FIVE

ON THE OTHER side of the portal, it was raining, and a cold wind blew through the bare trees.

Ray led Drew straight to ***Cruel School***. Instead of green grass, the yard was just dirt and rocks. Instead of a smiling face on the front door, there was a ***frowning*** face with shifty, ***mean*** eyes. And instead of bright, cheerful

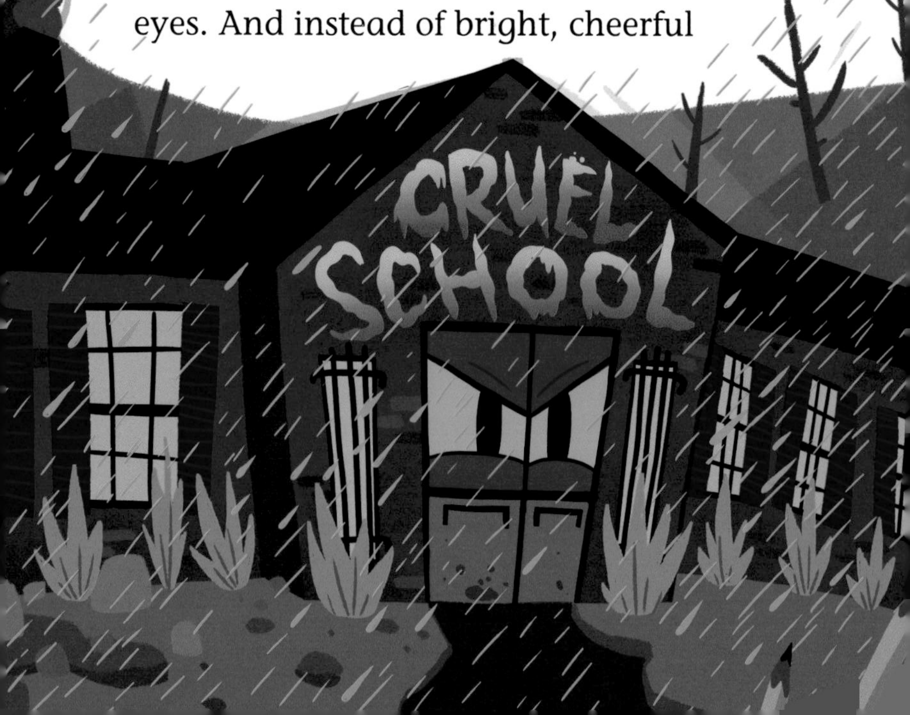
CRUEL
SCHOOL

colors, everything was painted in ***dark, depressing*** colors like gray, black, and muddy brown. Over the front door, ***CRUEL SCHOOL*** was spelled out in big letters.

"This is it," Ray said.

"Yeah, I figured," Drew said, looking up at the sign.

"Come on inside and meet my friends," Ray said, leading the way through the front doors.

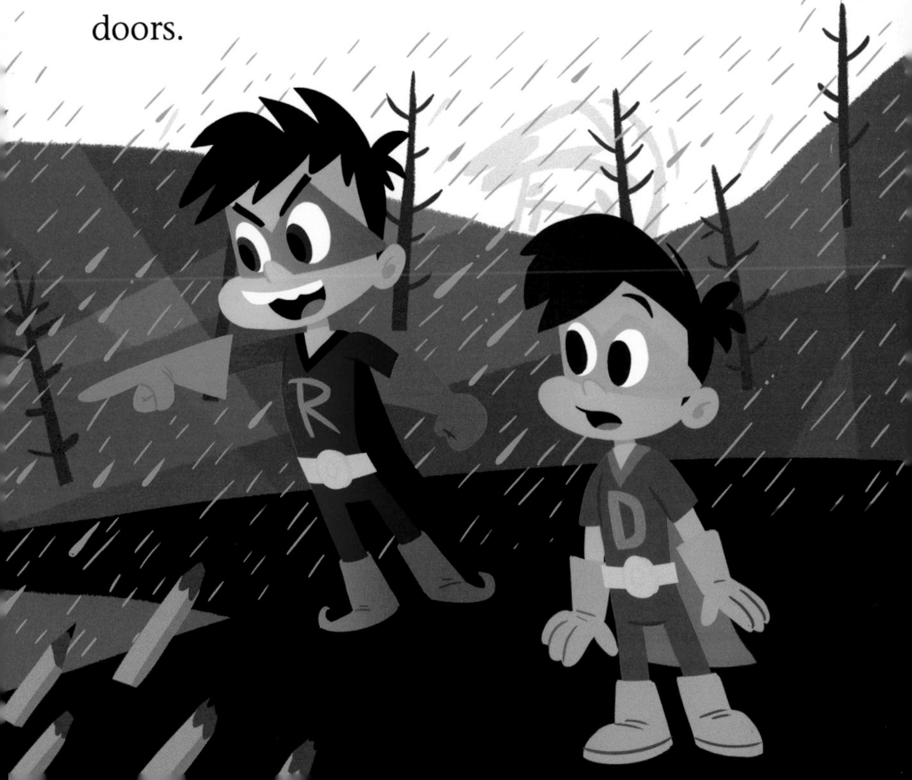

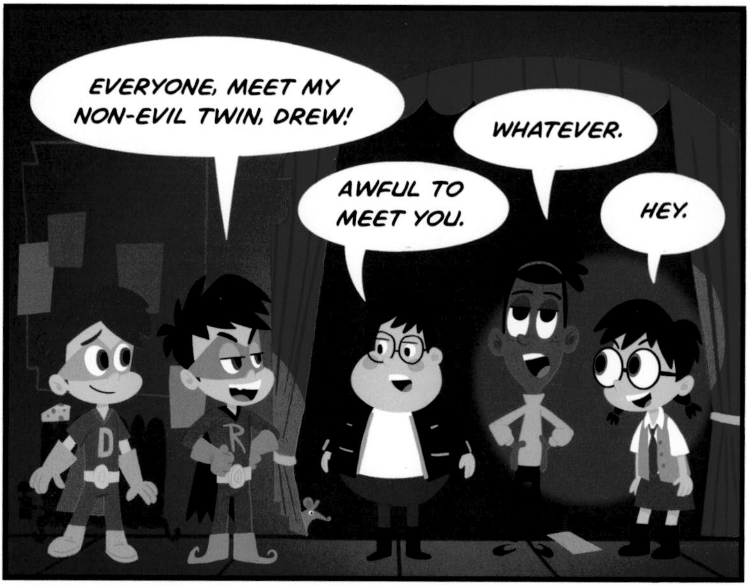
EVERYONE, MEET MY NON-EVIL TWIN, DREW!
AWFUL TO MEET YOU.
WHATEVER.
HEY.

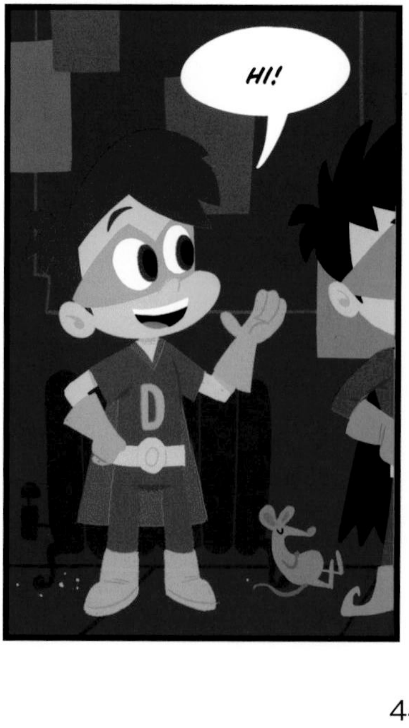
HI!

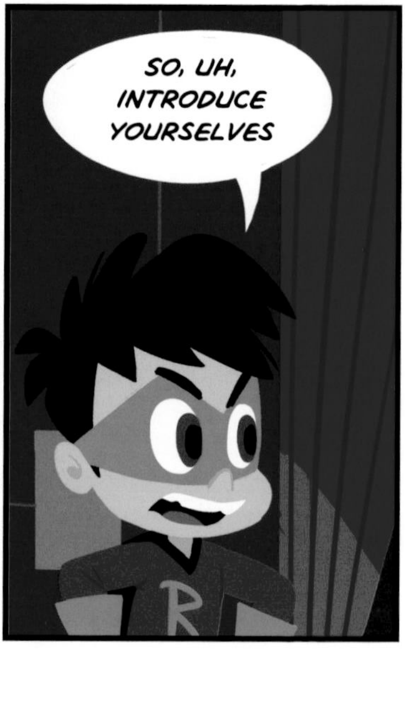
SO, UH, INTRODUCE YOURSELVES

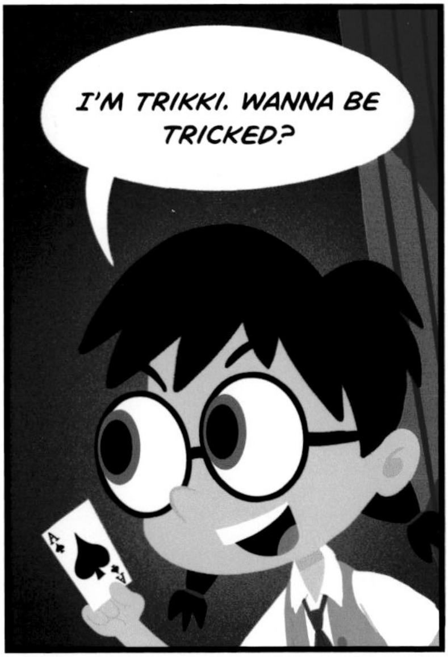
I'M TRIKKI. WANNA BE TRICKED?

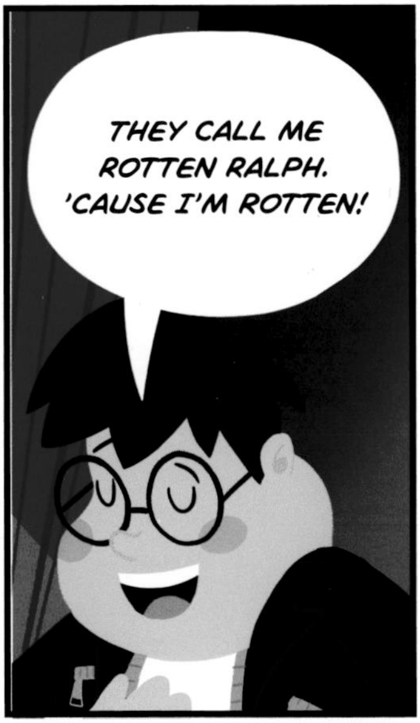
THEY CALL ME ROTTEN RALPH. 'CAUSE I'M ROTTEN!

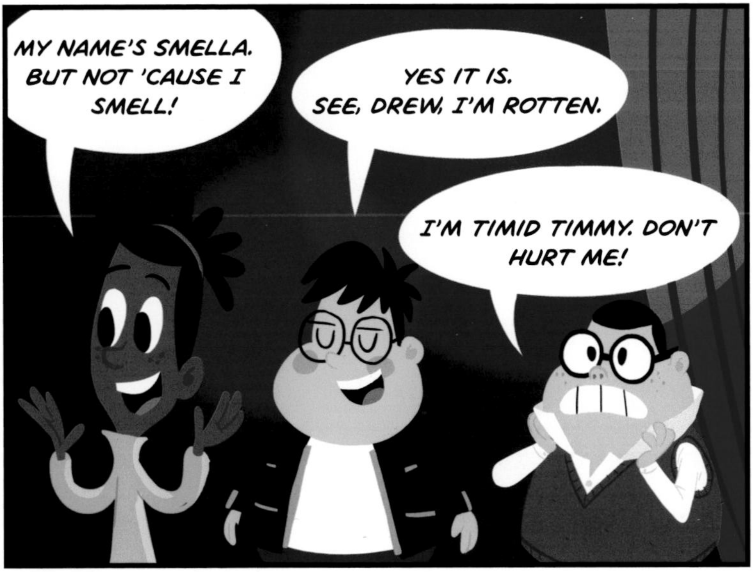
MY NAME'S SMELLA. BUT NOT 'CAUSE I SMELL!
YES IT IS. SEE, DREW, I'M ROTTEN.
I'M TIMID TIMMY. DON'T HURT ME!

After he'd introduced Drew to his friends, Ray took him on a tour of Cruel School. **"Come on,"** he said. "I'll show you how ***terrible*** everything is here."

"Sounds fun," Drew said, trying to make a joke.

"Oh, don't worry," Ray assured him. "It won't be."

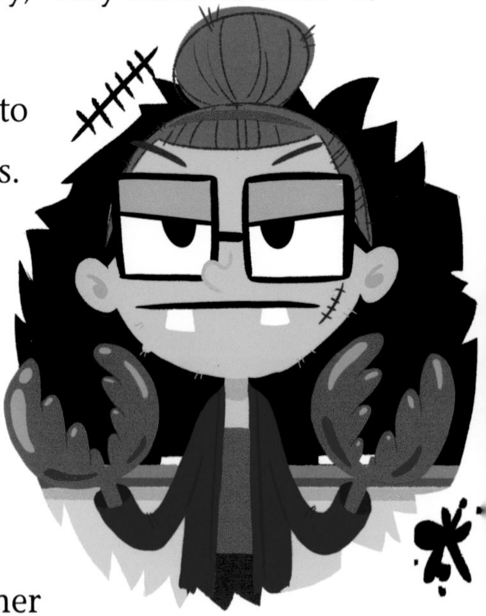

First they went to arts and crafts class. The teacher was named ***Crabby Carol.*** She looked a little like Drew's teacher, Crafty Carol. But she had a scar on her face and buckteeth, and instead of normal hands, she had red claws!

"Who's this?" she snapped when she saw Drew.

"Drew," Ray answered. "My non-evil twin. I'm showing him ***Cruel School."***

Crabby Carol made everyone start working on the day's craft project: making slime. At first, Drew thought it'd be fun to make slime. ***"Making slime?"*** he whispered to Ray. "We do that at Cool School, too! ***It's fun!"***

"Just wait," Ray warned.

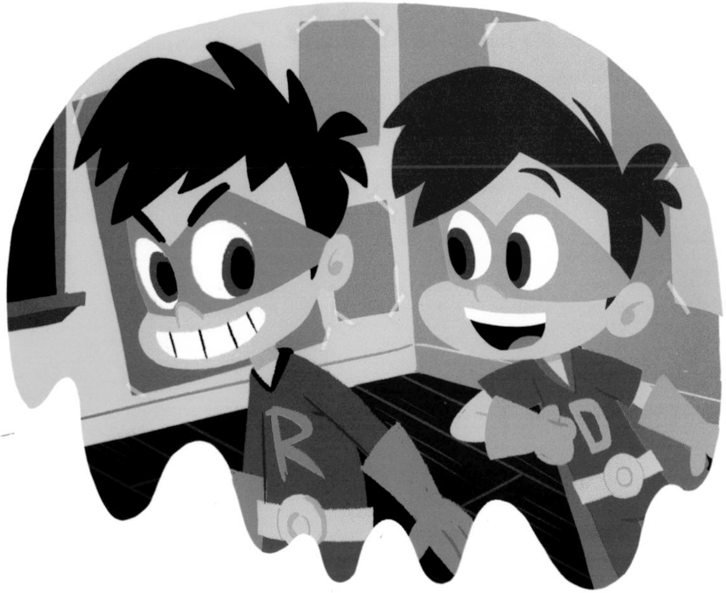
R
D

He was right. Crabby Carol brought out the ingredients for making the slime; they were all totally disgusting! ***Mold! Mildew! Mucus! Ear wax! Boogers! Dead slugs!***

"*Ew,*" Drew said, holding his nose.

"What'd I tell you?" Ray said.

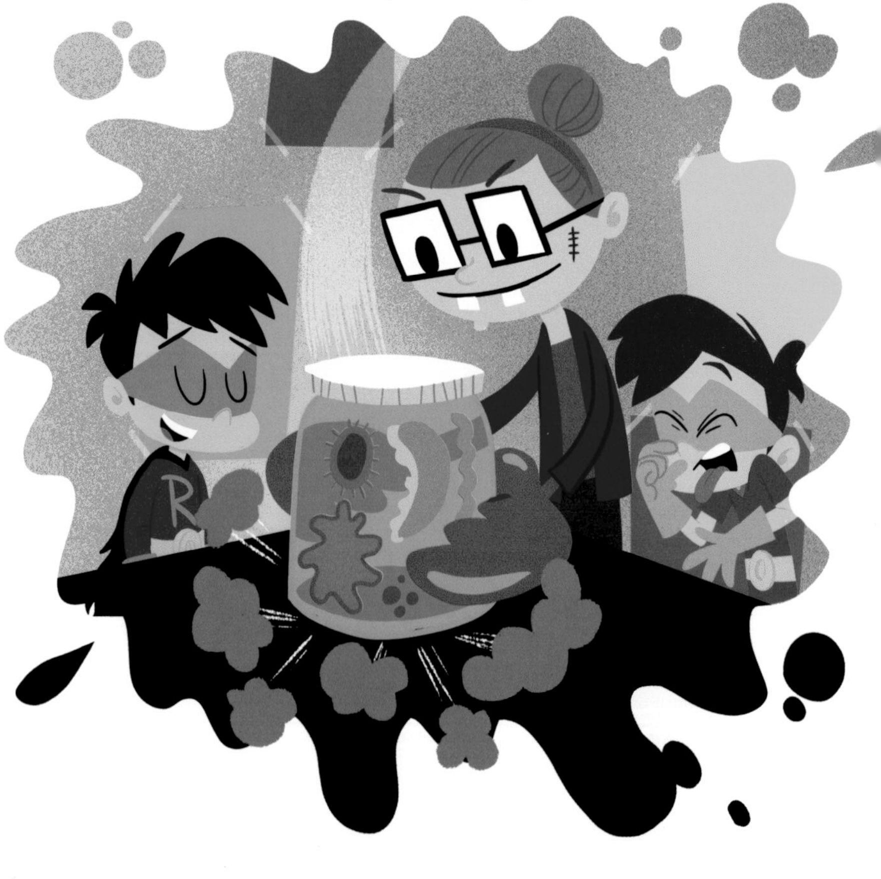
R

Crabby Carol made the students combine the gross ingredients. All mixed together, they made a ***horrible slime*** that stuck to everything.

"Slime is supposed to be smooth and slippery," Drew complained. "This stuff is way too sticky!"

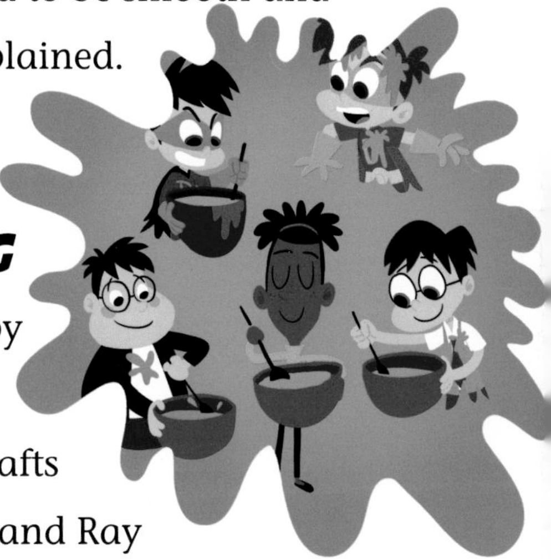

"NO TALKING IN CLASS!" Crabby Carol shouted.

When arts and crafts class was over, Drew and Ray hurried out of the stinky room, still trying to wipe the sickening slime off their hands and clothes.

"Where to next?" Drew asked.

"The library," Ray said.

"Oh, I love libraries!" Drew enthused.

"You won't love this one," Ray promised.

CHAPTER SIX

WHEN DREW first entered the library and saw the librarian from behind, he thought he recognized her. ***"Ms. Booksy?"*** he said, amazed to find the Cool School librarian in Cruel School.

But when she turned around, Drew instantly saw that she was ***NOT*** Ms. Booksy! This librarian had a black patch over one eye. And instead of hands, she had hooks!

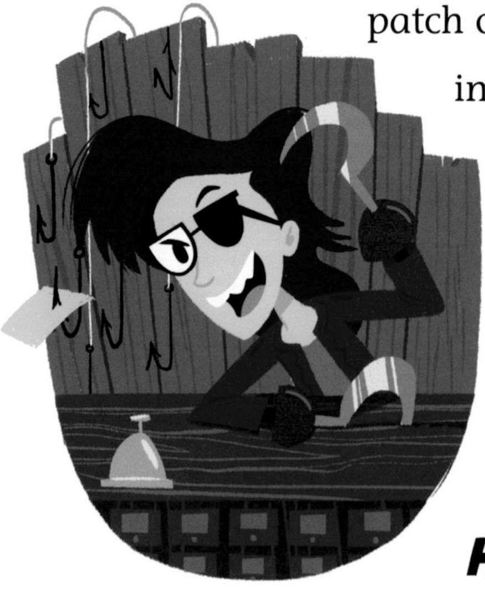

"What did you call me?" she snarled. ***"My name is Captain Hooksy!"***

The librarian seemed angry, so Drew tried to be extra-nice to make her feel better. ***"Oh, I'm sorry,"*** he said. "You know, in our library today we made up a really funny story about a pirate sailing in a bathtub. . . ."

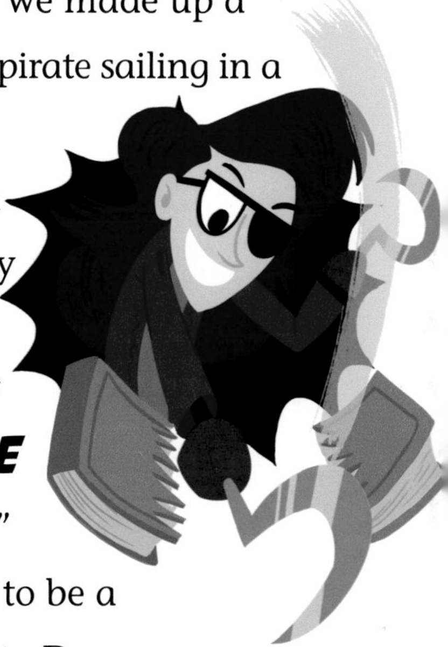

"Pirates do NOT sail in bathtubs!" Captain Hooksy shrieked, slicing her hook right through the pages of a book. ***"Pirates HATE baths!*** I ought to know."

"Captain Hooksy used to be a pirate," Smella whispered to Drew.

"Oh," Drew said. "I guess that makes sense. Sort of."

As lightning flashed outside the library windows, Captain Hooksy ordered the students to sit down so she could read them a story.

"Are you going to use **funny voices** when you read?" Drew asked eagerly. He always thought it was hilarious when Ms. Booksy changed her voice for each character in a story.

"What are you saying?" Captain Hooksy growled. "Do you think my voice is *funny*?"

Drew shook his head rapidly. ***"No, not at all,"*** he said. "Of course not. Your voice isn't at all funny."

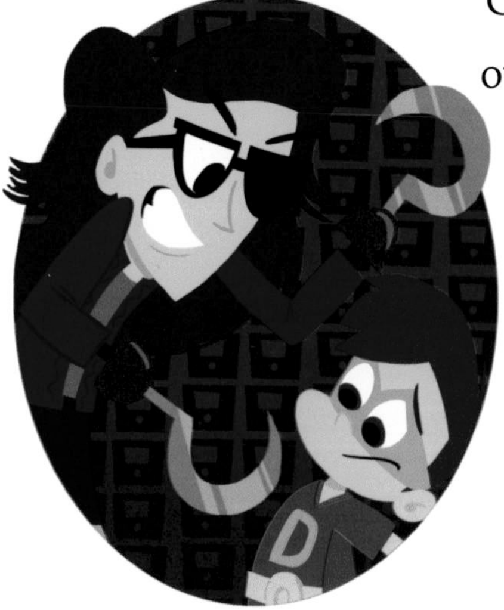

Captain Hooksy leaned over, putting her face close to Drew's. "Well, you better not say my voice is funny, or you'll be walking the plank!"

Drew gulped.

The librarian snatched a book off the shelf and started to read, using her hooks to rip right through each page after she finished reading it.

She read *Snow White the Seven Dwarfs*, but at the end of the story, the evil queen won!

"What?!" Drew couldn't help but exclaim. ***"That's not how it ends!"***

"The story ends the way *I say* it ends!"
Captain Hooksy insisted. She tore the
last piece of the book to shreds. Then she
grabbed another book and furiously read
more stories, each one ending with the bad
guys winning.

"But ***the good guys*** should win,"
Drew protested.

"Not in MY library!" Captain Hooksy
screamed. ***"CLASS DISMISSED!"***

As they walked out of the library, Drew said to Ray, "Boy, I see what you mean. It really is **pretty bad** here at Cruel School."

"Yeah," Ray said in his raspy voice. "And you haven't even met Dean Mean yet."

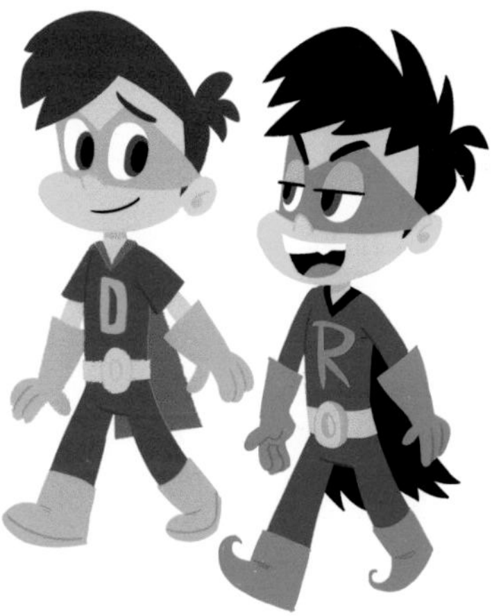
D
R

"Dean Mean?" Drew asked. "Who's that?"

Suddenly, a low-pitched voice bellowed from down the hall, **"RAY BLANK, GET OVER HERE!"**

"Oops," Ray said nervously. **"Looks like you're about to meet him!"**

CHAPTER SEVEN

"I'M WARNING YOU, RAY BLANK!" Dean Mean yelled down the Cruel School hallway. "YOU **GET OVER HERE** RIGHT THIS INSTANT . . . OR ELSE!!!"

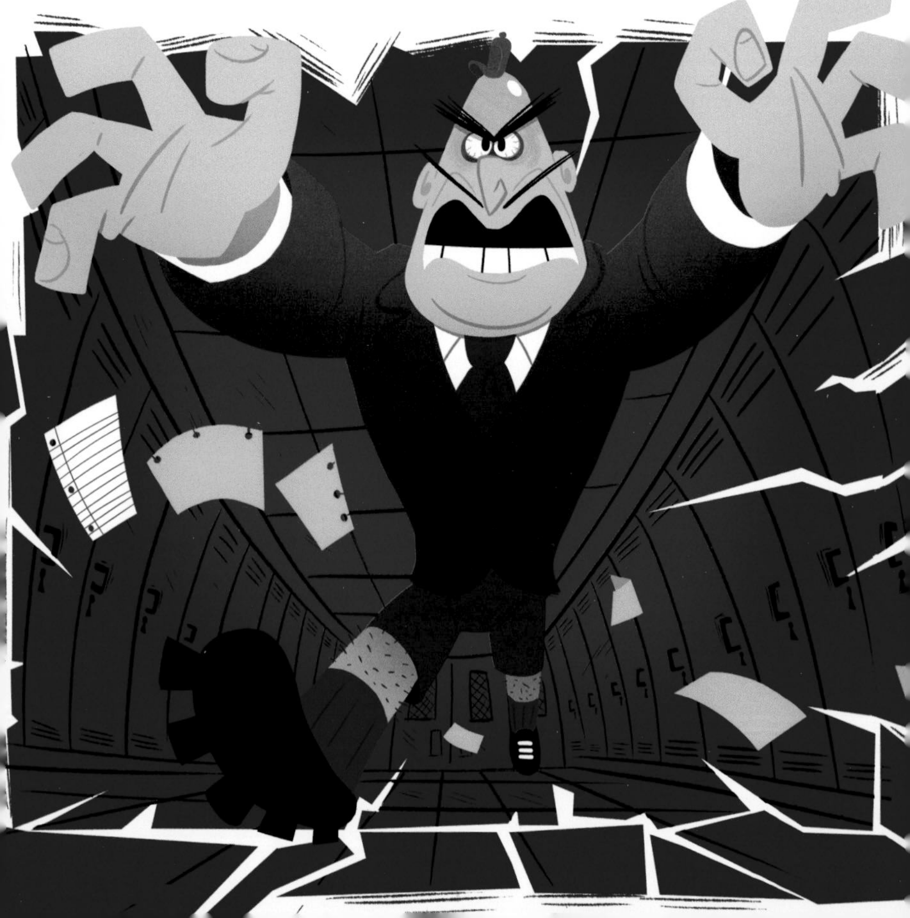

The dean of Cruel School, ***Dean Mean***, was a big man with a long black mustache and bushy black eyebrows. He wore a gray jacket, a green tie, a little purple-and-green cap, purple socks, and green shorts that showed his hairy legs.

He stormed down the hall straight toward Ray and Drew!

"We gotta hide!" Ray hissed. He dove into the nearest locker, shutting the door behind him. Drew looked around for a good hiding place, but it was too late. Dean Mean stomped right up to him and leaned over, sticking his grouchy face right in Drew's. "Ray Blank! What are you doing out here in the hallway? ***GET BACK TO CLASS!"***

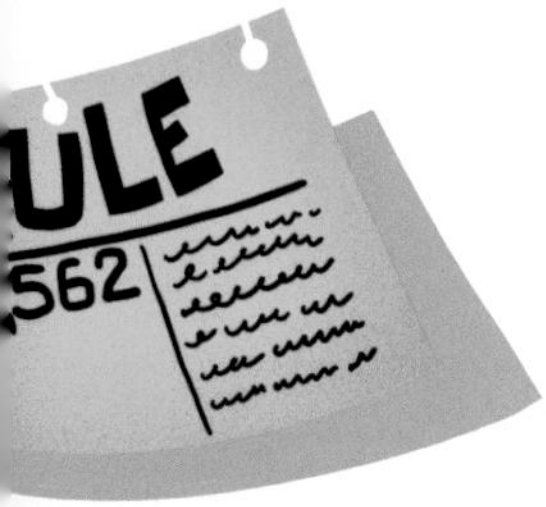
ULE
562

"Um, Dean Mean, you're actually making a mistake," Drew said nervously. **"I'M WHAT?!"** Dean Mean roared. **"WHAT DID YOU SAY?!"**

Drew gulped and spoke up a little louder. "I said, you're making a mistake. **I'm not Ray Blank**. He's my evil twin. **My name is Drew Pendous**, and I don't even go to Cruel School. I go to Cool School."

Dean Mean stared at Drew for a second. Then he burst out laughing. **"HA HA HA!** You think I don't know what my own students look like? Nice try! Now come with me, Ray."

The head of Cruel School put his big hand on Drew's shoulder, gripped it tightly, and started marching him down the hall. From inside the locker, Ray heard everything.

Oh wow! he thought to himself. As soon as he heard Dean Mean and Drew walking away, Ray quietly opened the locker door and slipped down the hallway in the opposite direction!

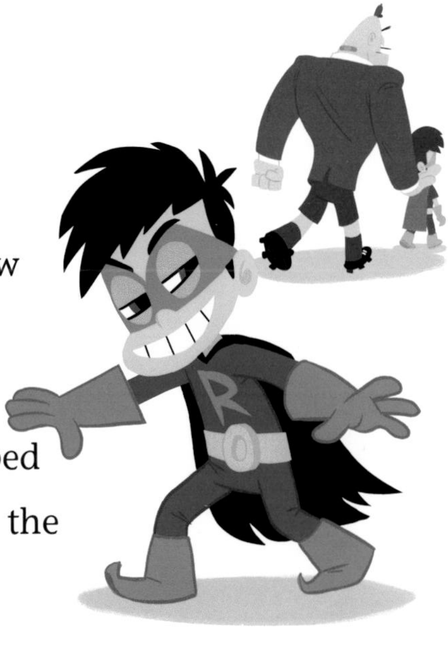

Drew didn't much like being led away by Dean Mean. He wriggled free. Then he pulled out his mighty Pen Ultimate and started to draw a portal back to Cool School on the hallway wall. If he could just finish drawing the portal, then he could open the door and jump through. Then he'd be back in Cool School, where he belonged!

"HEY!" Dean Mean barked. **"NO GRAFFITI ALLOWED!"**

He rushed toward Drew and snatched his Pen Ultimate away. "I'm locking this graffiti pen in my office. Now ***GET BACK TO CLASS IMMEDIATELY!"***

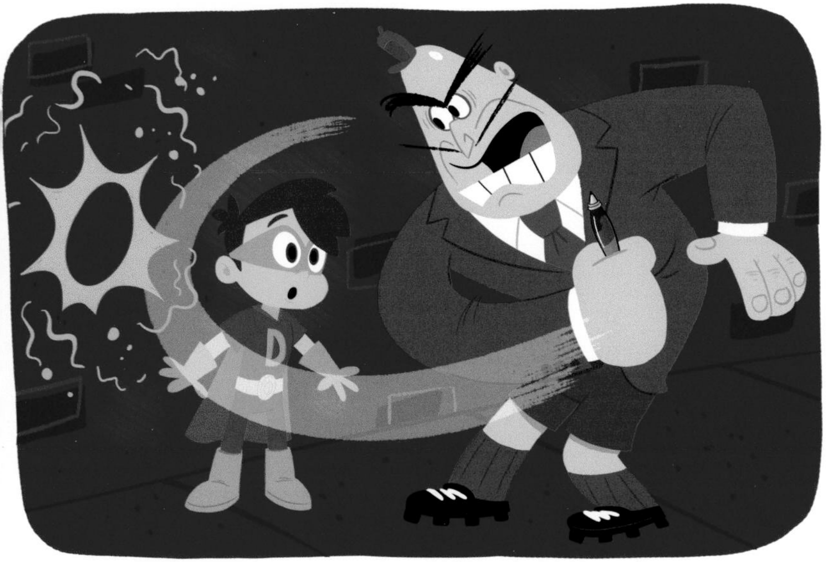
D

Dean Mean clomped off down the hallway to his office, carrying Drew's pen. Drew pretended he was going into a classroom but then turned around and sneaked back to the locker where Ray had been hiding.

"Ray?" he whispered. ***"Ray? You can come out now! He's gone!"***

Drew opened the locker door. Empty! Ray was gone!

"Looks like I'll have to get my ***Pen Ultimate*** back all by myself!" Drew said with great determination. He headed off down the hall toward Dean Mean's office.

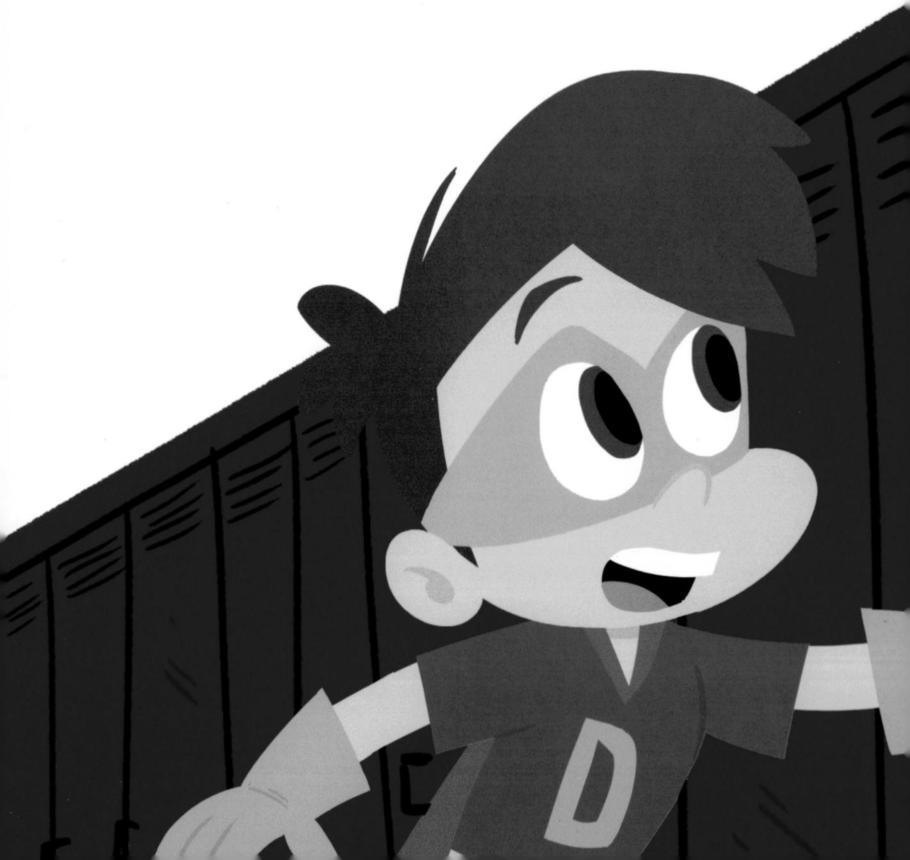
D

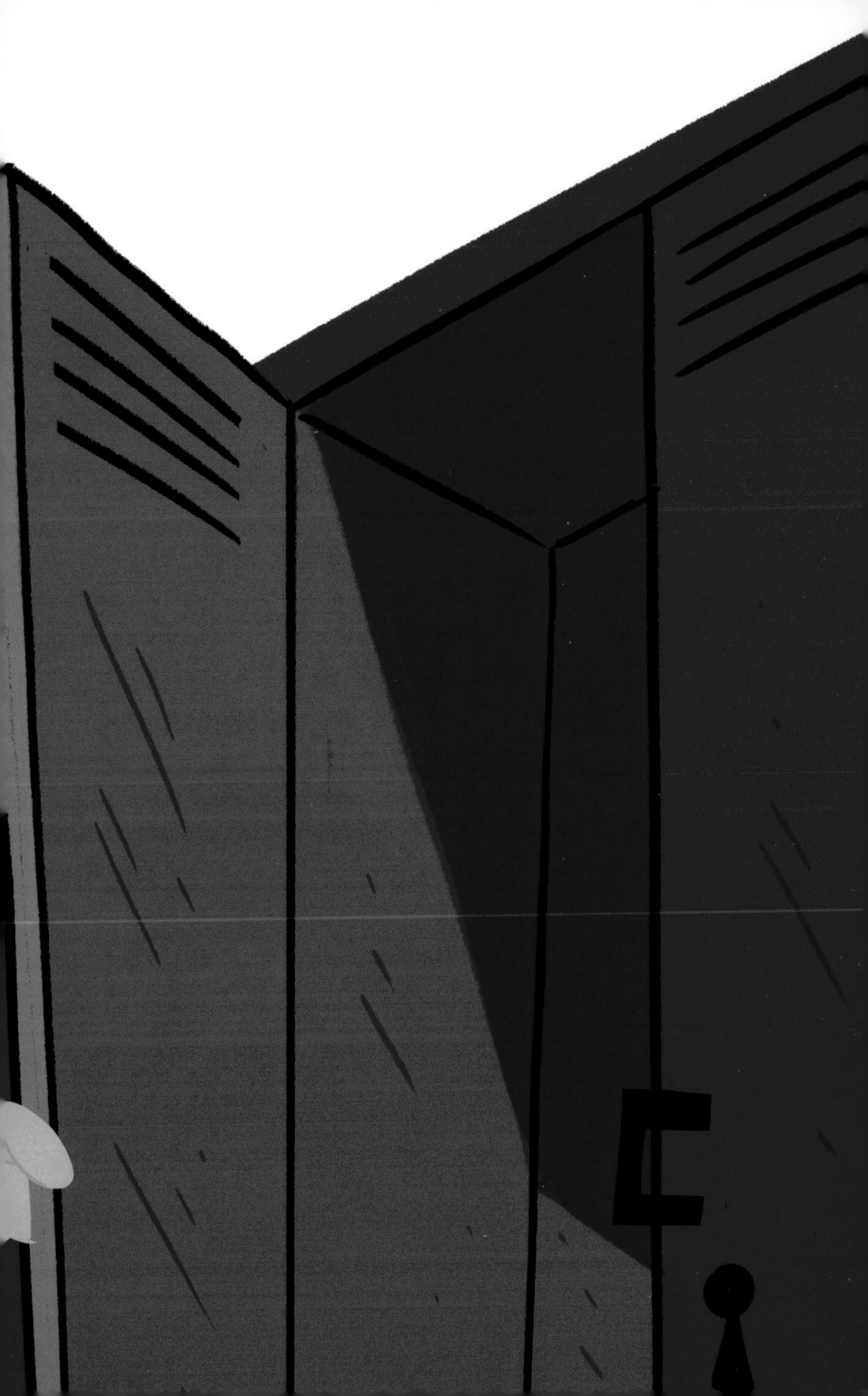

CHAPTER EIGHT

DREW TIPTOED down the hall, afraid that one of the mean Cruel School teachers would pop out of a classroom and grab him. But no one saw him.

After turning a couple of corners, he found a closed door with a sign on it that read ***DEAN MEAN'S OFFICE! KNOCK!*** Or better yet, ***GO AWAY!***

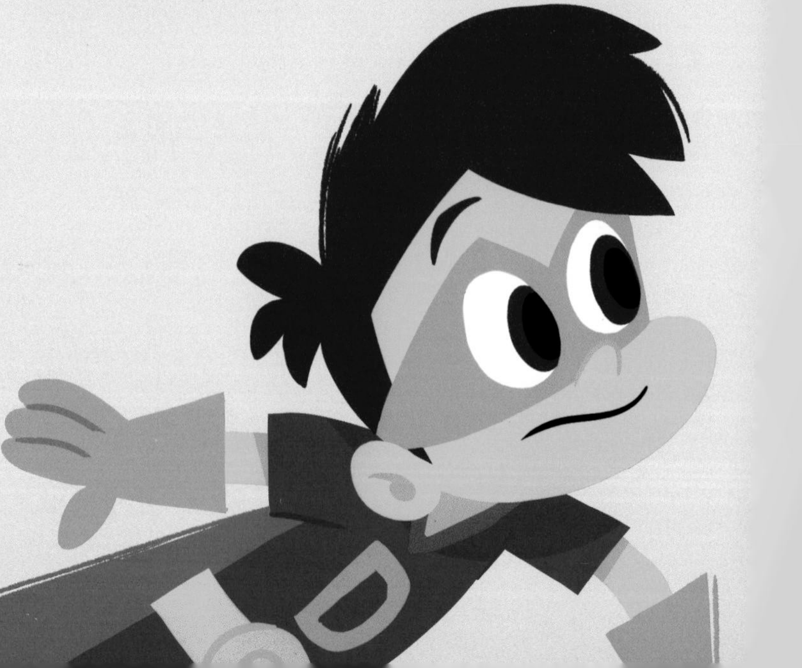

Drew put his ear up to the door and listened. ***He thought he heard snoring.***

Very slowly and carefully, Drew turned the doorknob, trying not to make a sound. When the knob wouldn't turn any more, he gently pulled the door open about an inch and peeked through the crack.

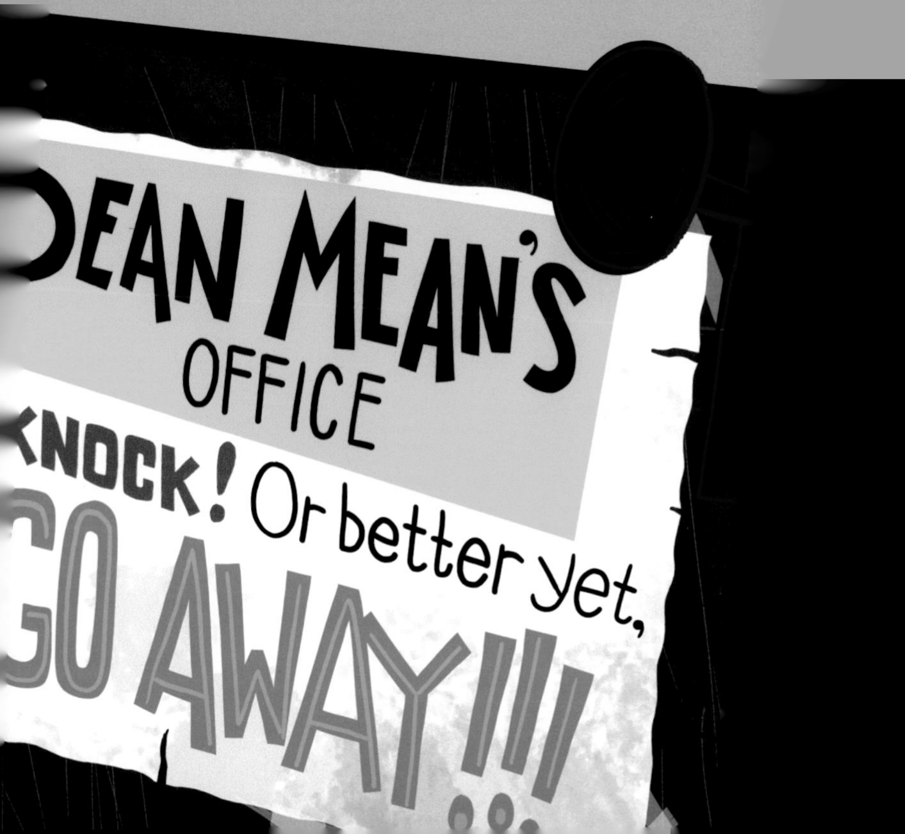
EAN MEAN'S
OFFICE
NOCK! Or better yet,
GO AWAY!!!

Dean Mean's office had lots of ***signs*** on the walls with ***long lists*** of Cruel School rules. There was a big wooden desk with a ***big chair*** behind it and a ***little chair*** in front of it, where students sat while the dean yelled at them for breaking school rules. And along one wall, there was a beat-up old brown couch.

Dean Mean was sleeping on the couch.

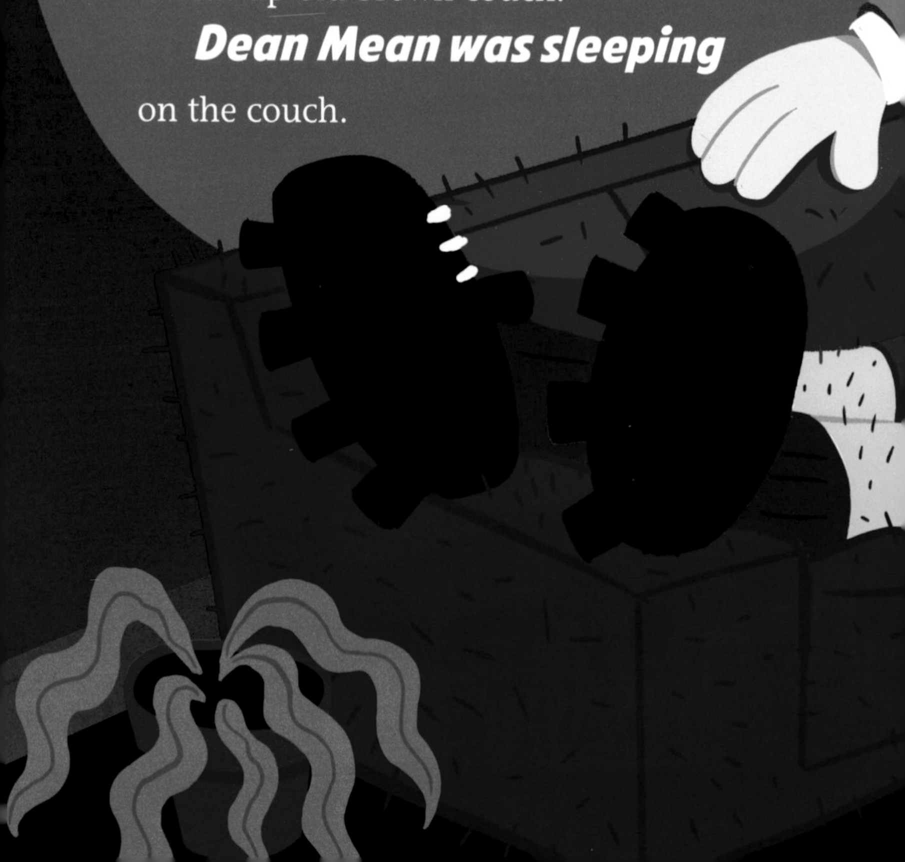

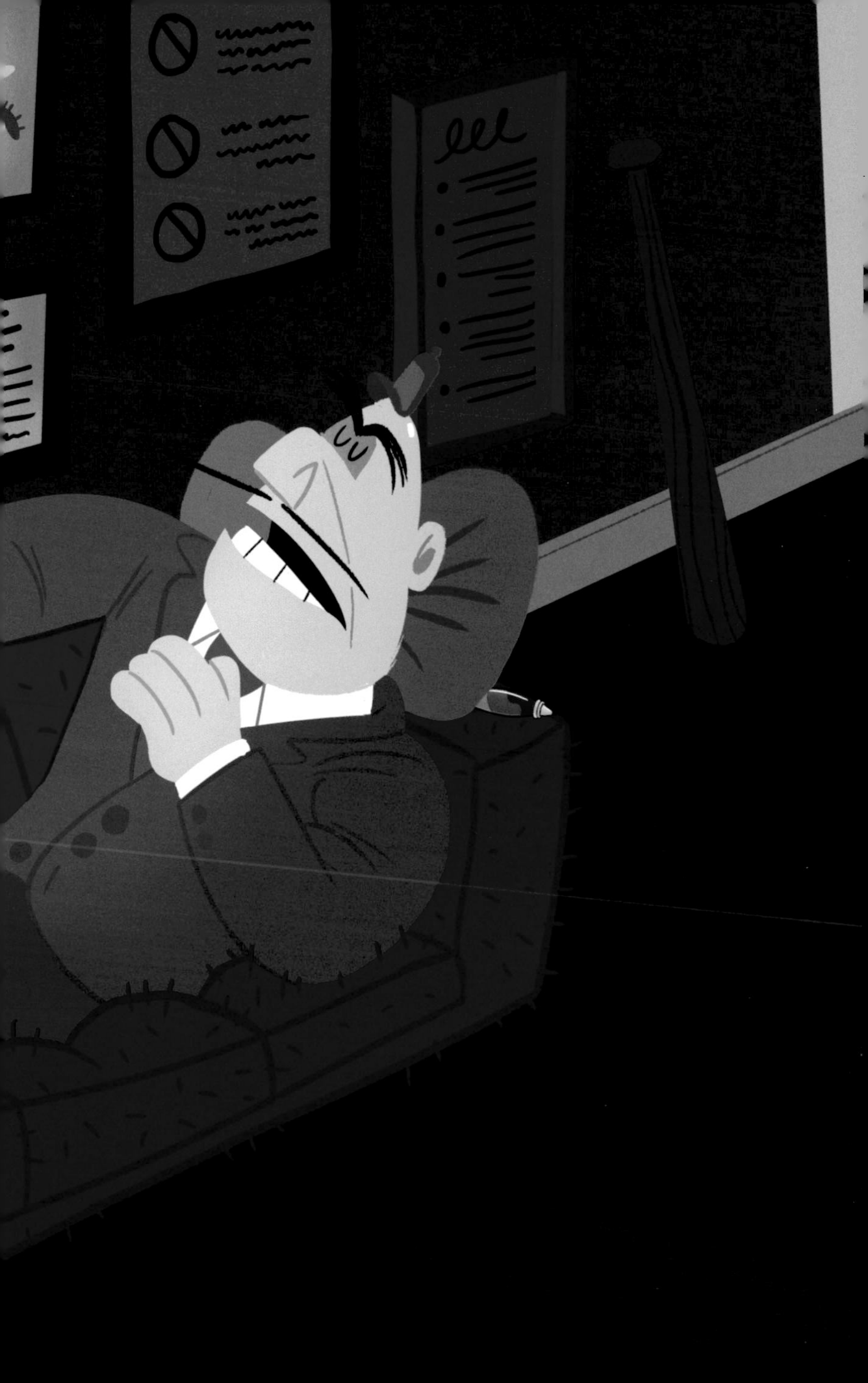

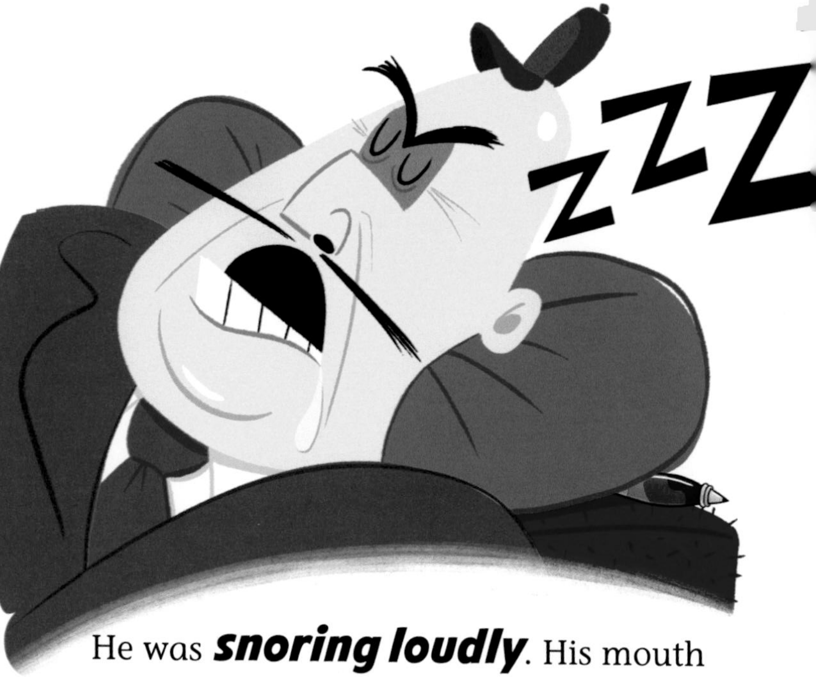
zZZ

He was ***snoring loudly***. His mouth was open, and a little drool had trickled down onto his chin. After he'd gotten back to his office, he'd decided it was a good time for a quick nap.

As quietly as possible, Drew opened the door just wide enough to slip into the office. Once inside, he looked around, hoping to spot his pen. Since Dean Mean had threatened to lock the pen away, he didn't have much hope of seeing it sitting out in the open. He was worried that maybe his **Pen Ultimate** was locked up in a secret safe. He looked at all the signs on the walls, wondering if one of them had a safe hidden behind it.

But then, out of the corner of his eye, he caught a flash of purple, green, blue, and yellow. His Pen Ultimate! There it was . . .

UNDER THE DEAN'S PILLOW!

Could he get his pen back without waking up Dean Mean?

He had to try. . . .

Drew wished he could draw some kind of **Super-Silent Sneaking Shoes** onto his feet, but to do that, he'd need his pen! Moving slowly, he tiptoed over to the couch. Dean Mean made a loud snorting noise! ***Was he waking up?!*** Drew froze, standing as still as a marble statue. Then he heard the dean snoring again.

Drew stretched out his hand, reaching for his **Pen Ultimate**. Dean Mean shifted, smiling in his sleep. *He's probably dreaming about being mean to students,* Drew thought.

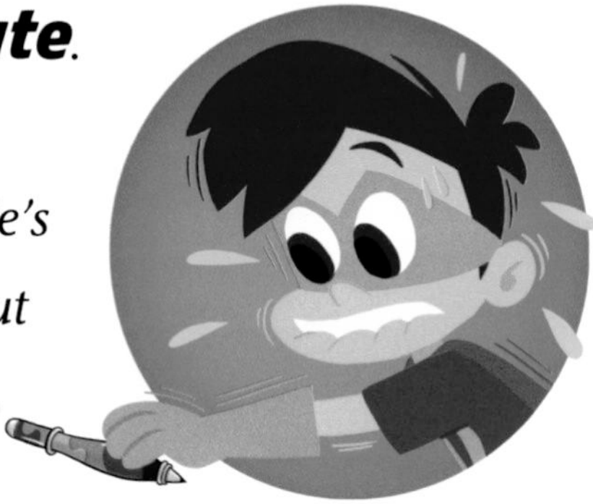

Finally, Drew's fingers were on the pen. Very, very slowly, he pulled his Pen Ultimate out from underneath Dean Mean's pillow. He had it! He turned to go . . .

. . . and stepped on a pencil some kid had

dropped on the floor! **"WHOA!"** Drew yelled as he slipped and fell with a crash. Dean Mean's eyes popped open! **"What?!** What's going on? Who's in my office?!" He looked around and saw Drew on the floor, holding his Pen Ultimate. **"YOU!"** the dean roared. "**RAY BLANK! GIVE ME BACK THAT GRAFFITI PEN!"**

Drew jumped to his feet and ran out of the office!

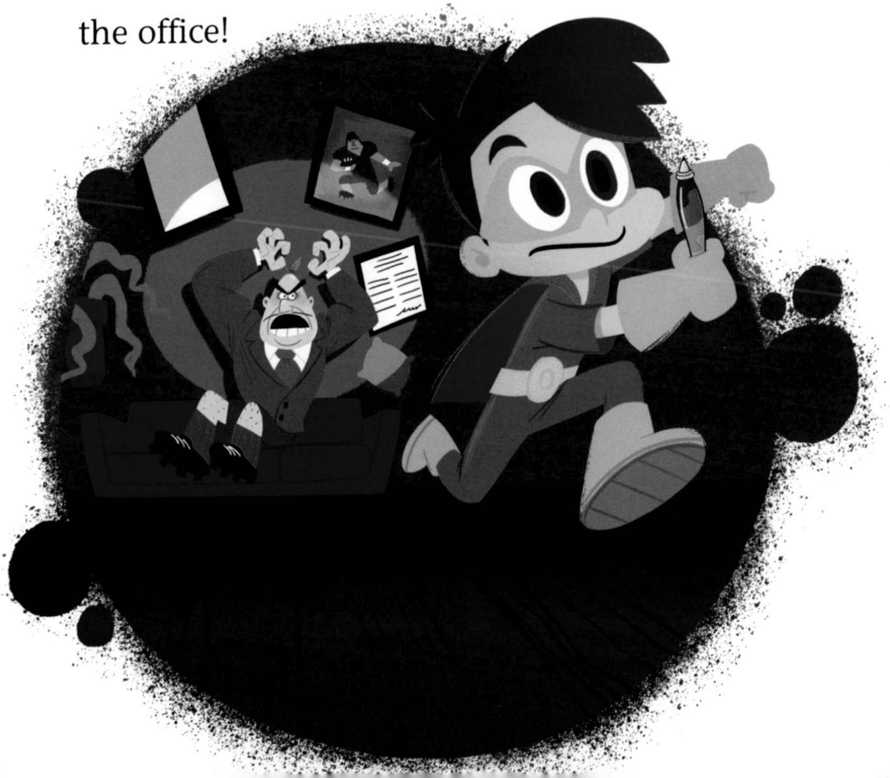

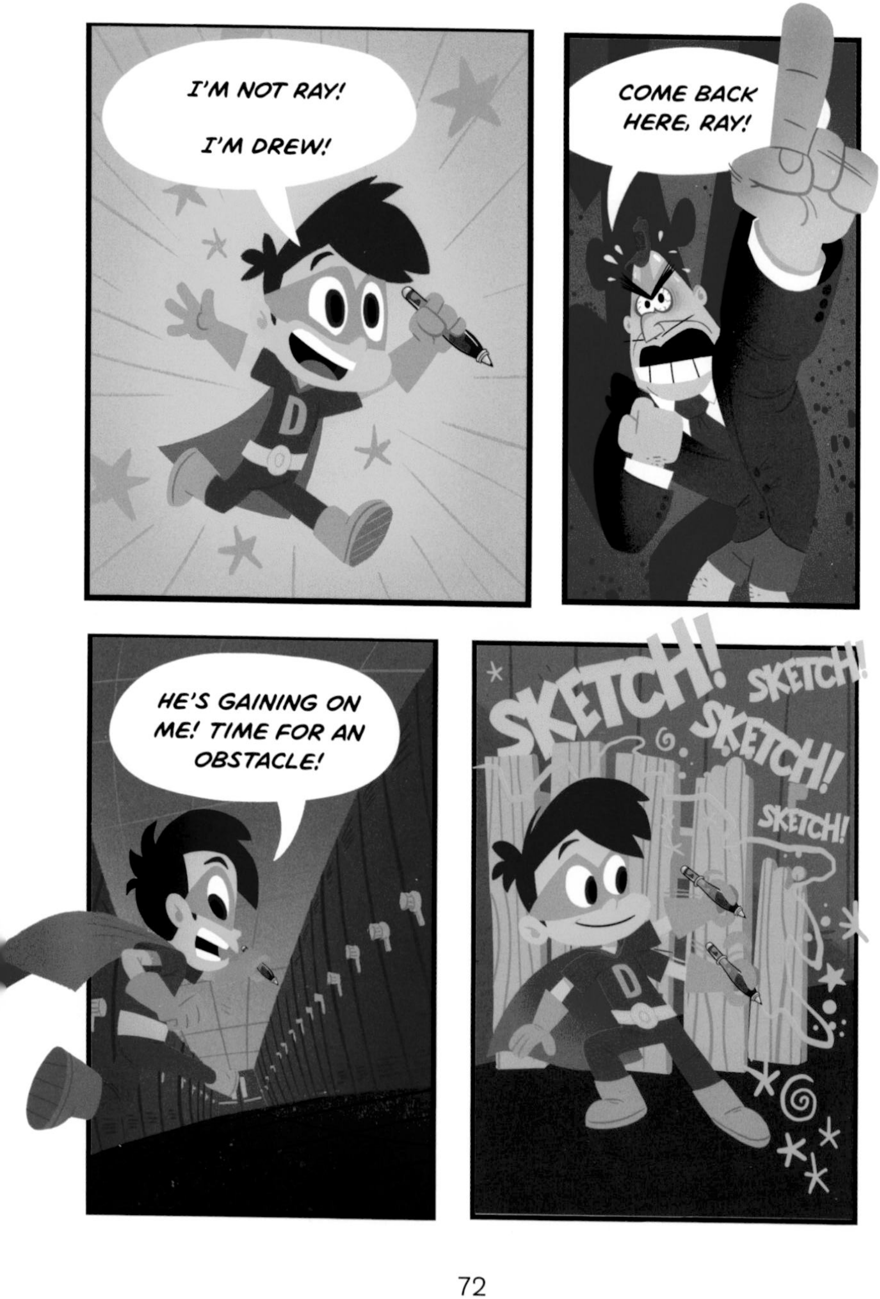
I'M NOT RAY!
I'M DREW!
COME BACK HERE, RAY!
HE'S GAINING ON ME! TIME FOR AN OBSTACLE!
SKETCH!
SKETCH!
SKETCH!
SKETCH!

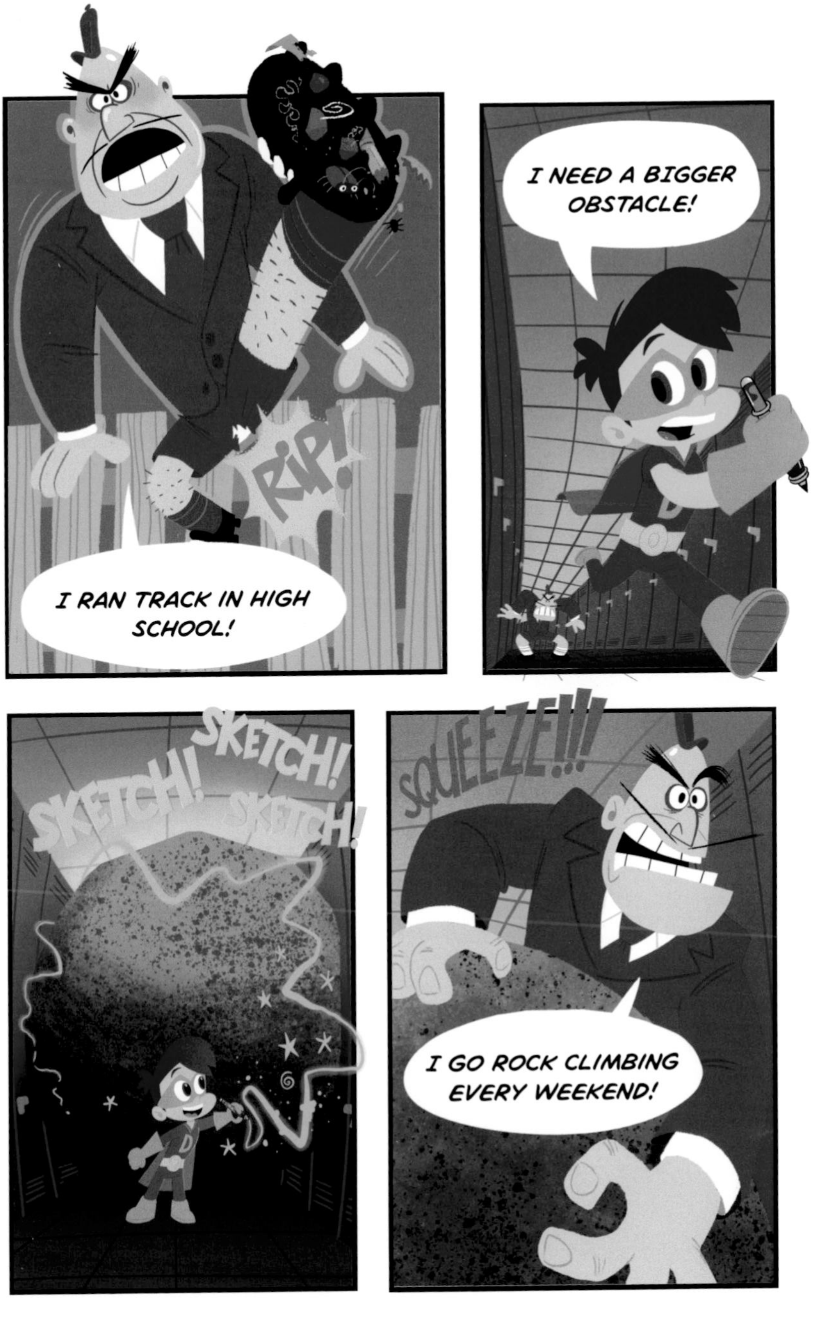
RIP!
I RAN TRACK IN HIGH SCHOOL!
I NEED A BIGGER OBSTACLE!
SKETCH! SKETCH! SKETCH!
SQUEEZE!!!
I GO ROCK CLIMBING EVERY WEEKEND!

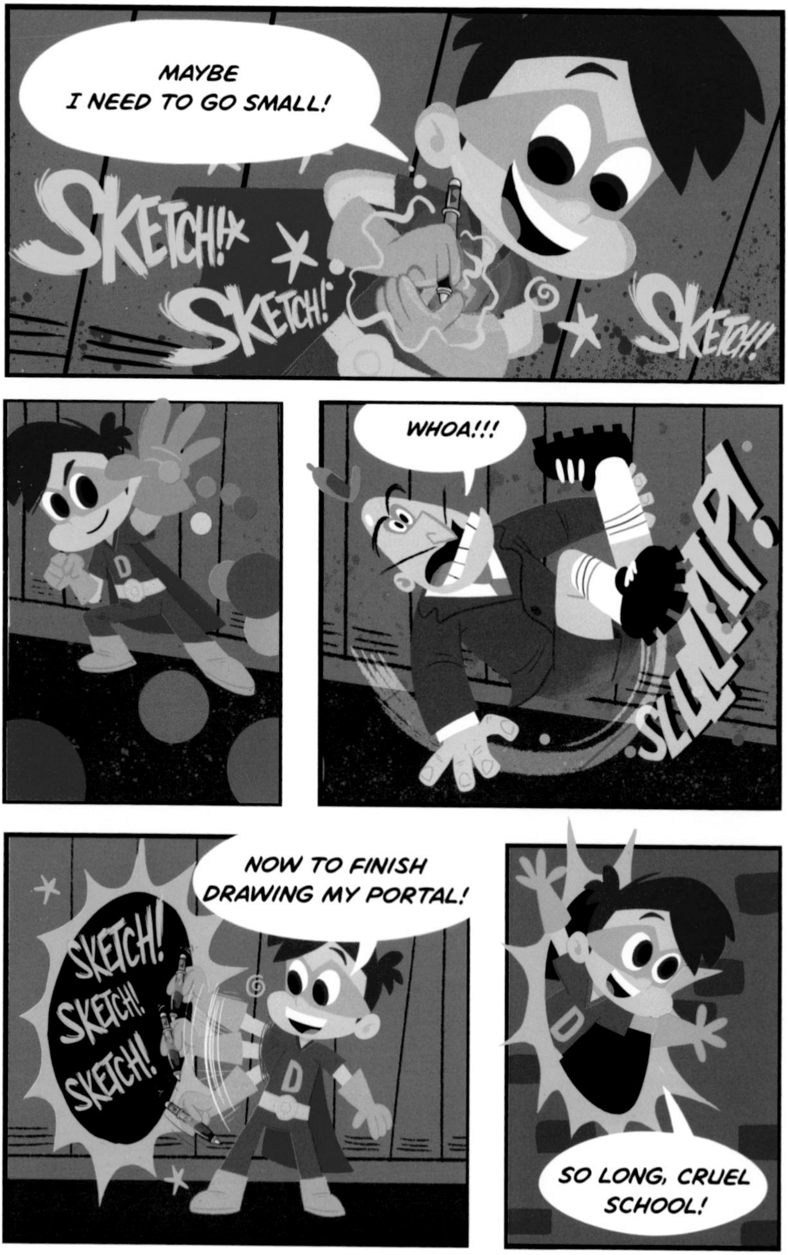
MAYBE I NEED TO GO SMALL!
SKETCH!!
SKETCH!
SKETCH!!
WHOA!!!
SLUMP!
NOW TO FINISH DRAWING MY PORTAL!
SKETCH! SKETCH! SKETCH!
SO LONG, CRUEL SCHOOL!

CHAPTER NINE

DREW WAS SO happy to be back in Cool School. It was about a billion times better than Cruel School.

But then he looked around.

Everything was a complete mess. Signs were missing letters! Lockers were missing doors! Ms. Booksy ran by, carrying a stack of books full of blank pages!

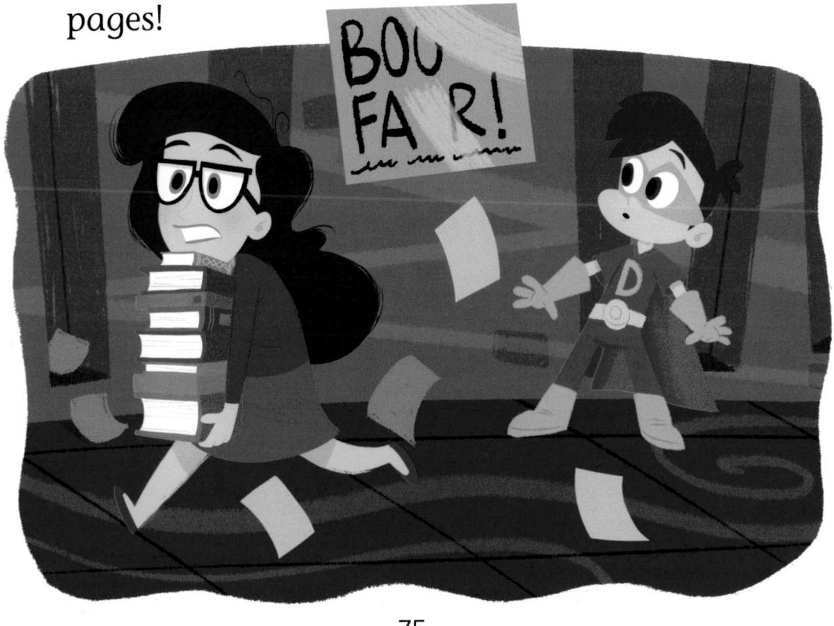
BOU
FA R!

"What is going on?!" Drew asked. He spotted Robby walking down the hallway with his hands out in front of him like a zombie, bumping into things.

"Robby!" Drew called. **"Are you a zombie?"**

"No," Robby said. "I don't think so. I just can't find my glasses."

Drew saw that Robby's glasses were missing. "What happened to them?"

"Somebody erased them," Robby explained. "He kind of looked like you, but his hair was black and his superhero costume was in different colors."

"Ray Blank!" Drew said. "He must have come back here! Did you see which way he went, Robby?"

Robby stopped and thought. "After he erased my glasses, it was hard for me to see anything. But I think I heard him head that way." Robby pointed down the hall and around a corner.

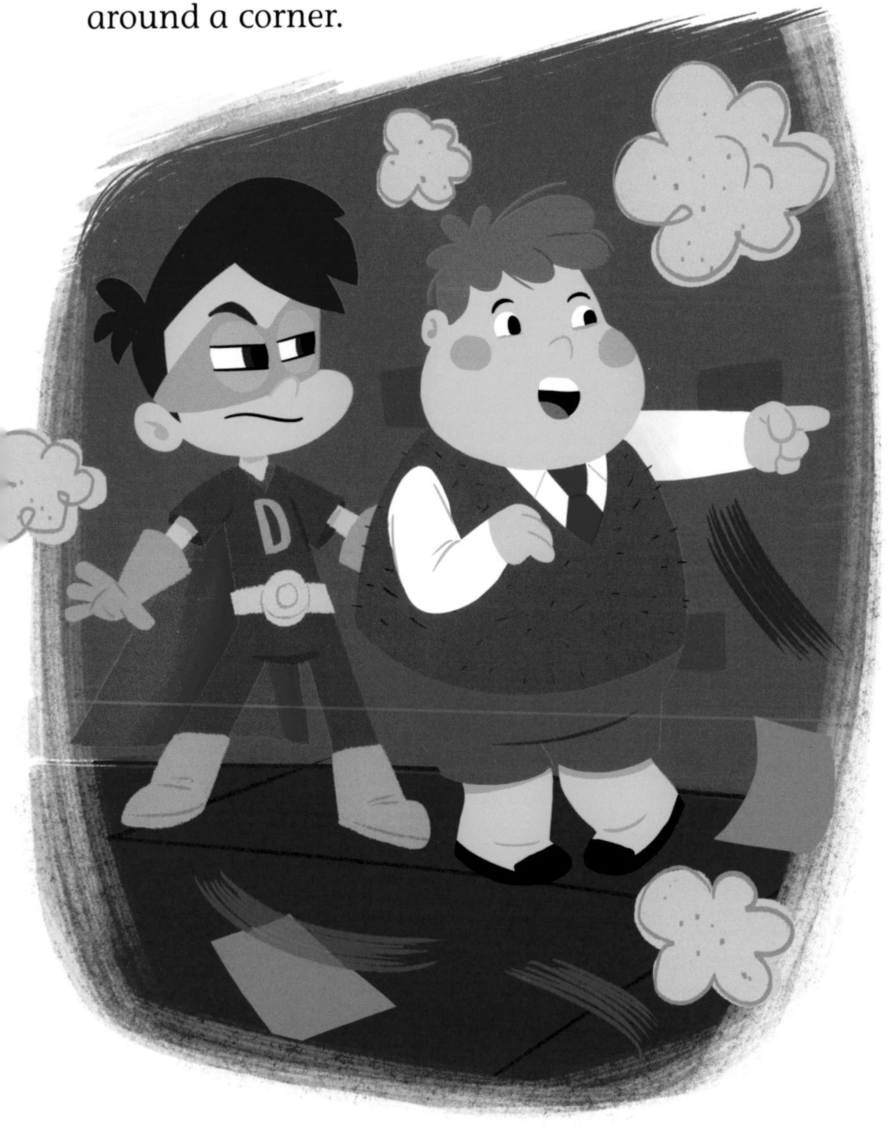

Drew ran down the hallway in the direction Robby was pointing. Around the corner, he could hear Ray's evil laugh. **"HA HA HA HA HA!"**

Ray was using his eraser to erase a drinking fountain.

That was terrible!

Everyone knew that Cool School had the most delicious cool water you could possibly find. So refreshing!

Drew ran right up to his evil twin. **"Ray! What are you DOING?!** Why are you erasing everything again? What happened to just wanting to be a student at Cool School?"

Ray shrugged. "I guess I just can't help myself. I'm a bad guy. Once an evil twin, always an evil twin! ***Next I'm going to erase your Pen Ultimate.***"

"Oh no you're not!" Drew said, taking off running. He got an idea and headed back toward his portal—the one that led back to Cruel School.

"Ha ha ha!" Ray laughed, chasing after Drew. "I'm just as fast as you are, Drew! ***I'm your twin,*** remember?"

Ray caught up with Drew near the portal back to Cruel School. "You're cornered, Drew! Give up! Where's that pen of yours?"

"I always keep it right here in my . . . pocket?" Drew said. He felt in his pocket, but it was empty. No pen! ***Where was his mighty Pen Ultimate?*** "Hey, where's my pen?"

Suddenly, Ray spotted the pen. It was lying on the ground on the other side of the portal! **"Aha!"** he cried triumphantly. **"There it is!"**

"Oh no!" Drew wailed. "I must have dropped it when I was jumping through the portal!" He hurried to retrieve his pen . . .

. . . but Ray dove past him and snagged

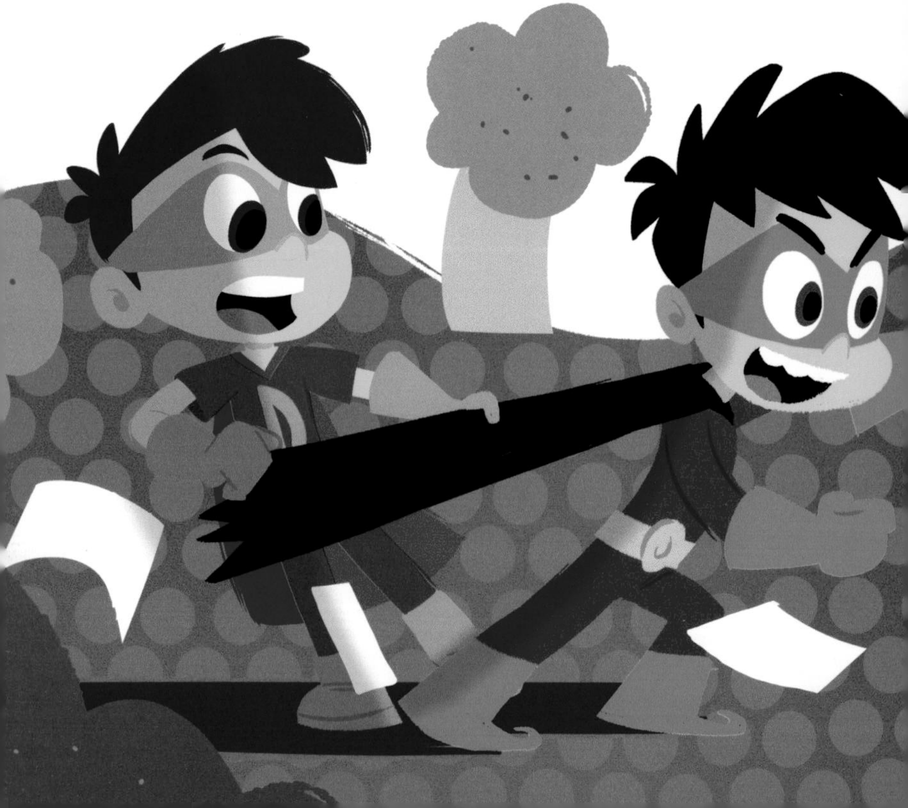

the pen! "It's my pen now! Ah ha ha! Now I can draw whatever I want **. . . AND TAKE OVER THE WORLD!**"

Ray decided the first thing he would draw would be a golden crown to wear as the new King of the World. He moved the Pen Ultimate through the air, but nothing happened.

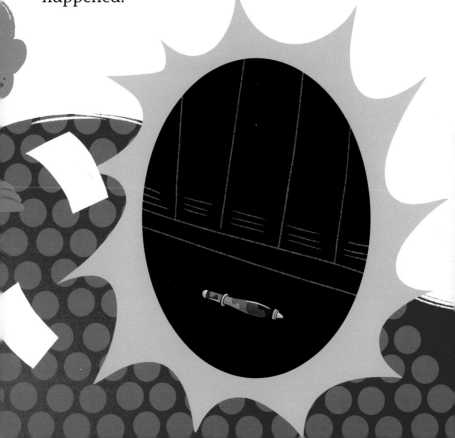

"Hey, wait a second!" he yelled. "This pen doesn't work."

"What's the matter, Ray?" Drew asked, smiling. ***"You drawing a blank?"***

Then Drew held up the ***REAL Pen Ultimate!*** He'd tricked Ray by drawing a

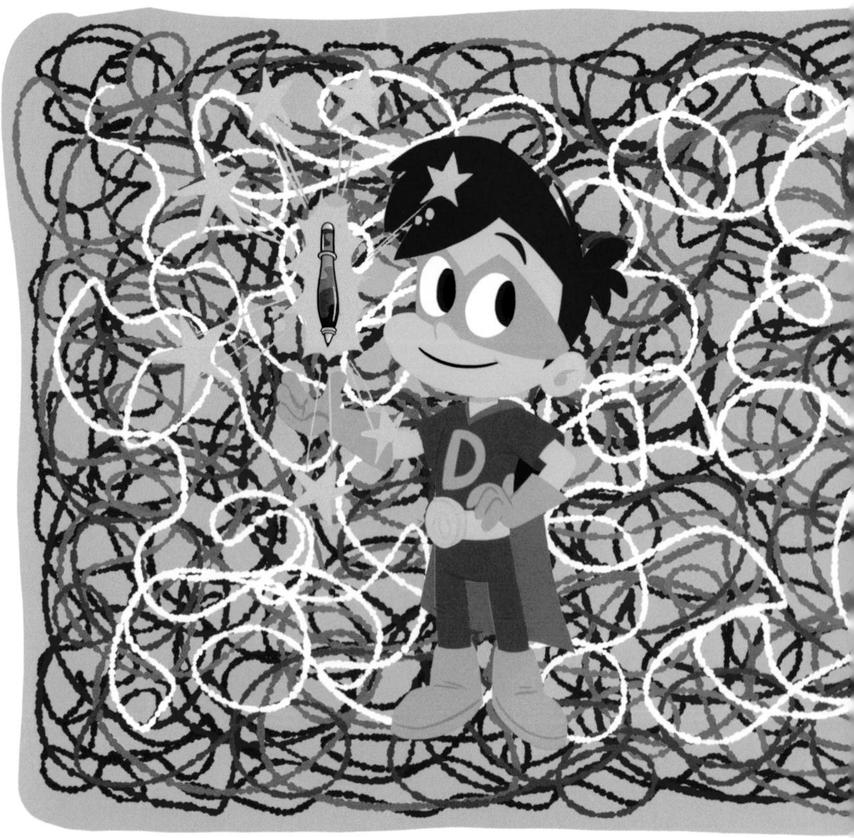

fake one that didn't work! He quickly drew a giant iron door over the portal and locked it, trapping Ray back in Cruel School.

"Whew!" Drew said. "That was a close one. And now to clean up this big mess!"

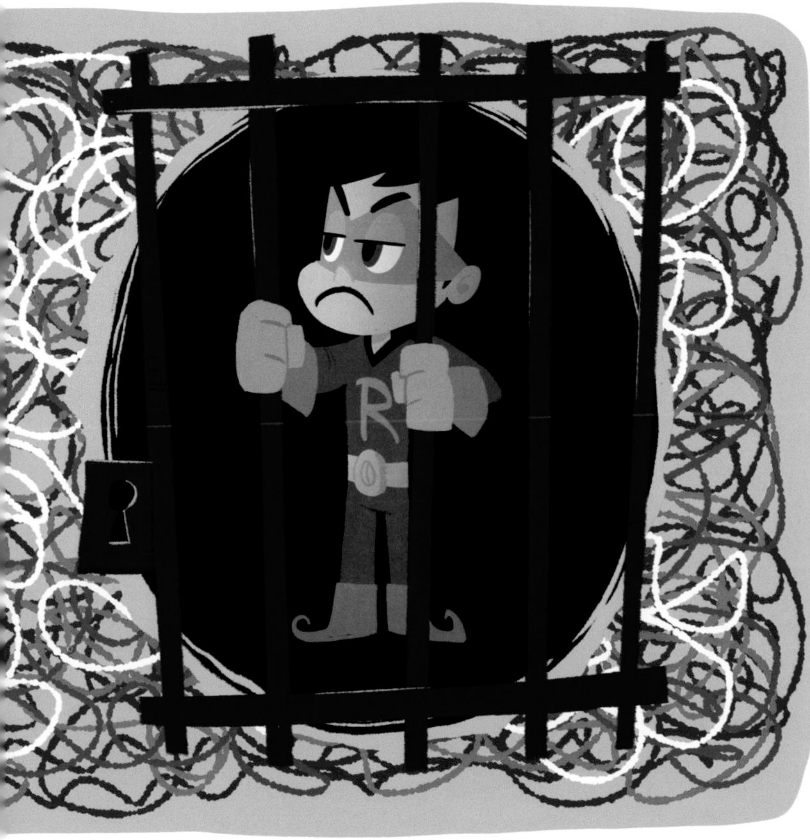
R

CHAPTER TEN

DREW HELPED clean up all the mess his evil twin had made.

In the science lab, he drew all the missing equipment that Ray had erased.

"Thanks, Drew!" Nikki said. "It was **TERRIBLE** not having all the equipment we need to do science experiments."

"No problem, Nikki!" Drew said. "Just let me know if you need anything else."

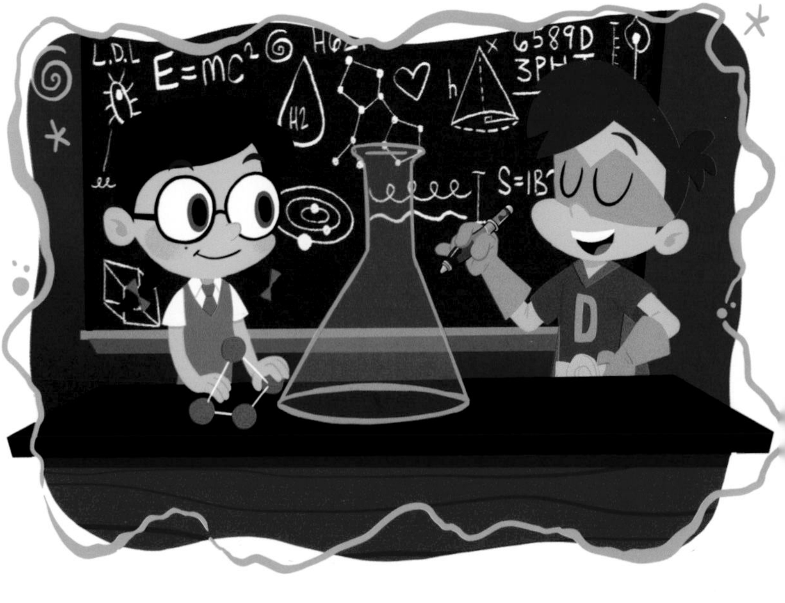
L.D.L
E=MC2
H2
6589D
3PH
S=IB
D

He also redrew Robby's glasses and
handed them to his friend. Robby put them
on and said, ***"Ah! I can SEE again!***
Thanks, Drew!"

"You're welcome!" Drew said.

To help Ms. Booksy fix all the library
books, Drew sketched lots and lots of pens.
Then he, Ella, and all the other Cool School
students helped write the missing words
back into the books.

"Maybe when we're done getting all these books back to normal, we'll write a **new book with our pirate story** in it," Ms. Booksy suggested. Everyone thought that was a great idea.

Out on the playground, Drew sketched new equipment: slides, swings, and monkey bars. **"Thanks, Drew!"** kids called to him as they ran toward the equipment to try it out.

In the cafeteria, Drew wrote **_pizza_**
and cake on the menu board. The lunch
lady was so grateful to have things back
the way they were supposed to be that she
happily whipped up lots of pizza and cake
for a celebration party! Everyone in Cool
School ate pizza and cake together and
had a great time.

But in **_Cruel School,_** Ray Blank was
NOT having a great time. . . .

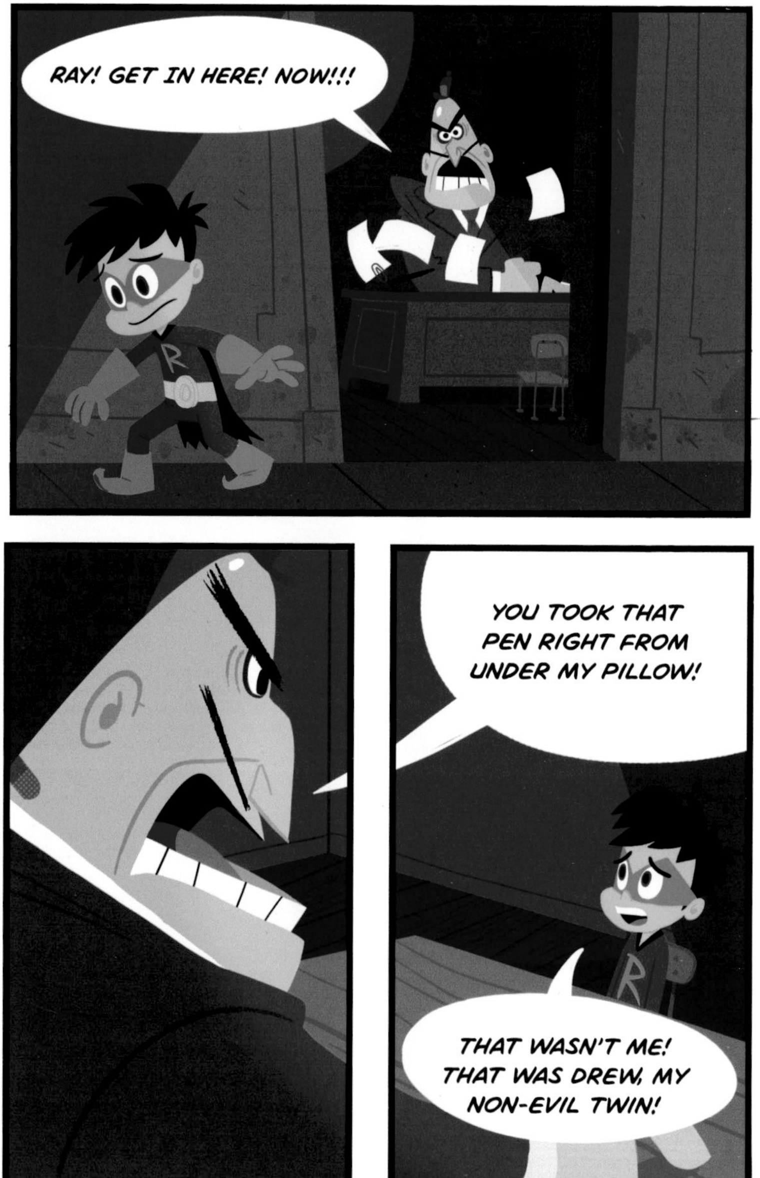
RAY! GET IN HERE! NOW!!!
YOU TOOK THAT PEN RIGHT FROM UNDER MY PILLOW!
THAT WASN'T ME! THAT WAS DREW, MY NON-EVIL TWIN!

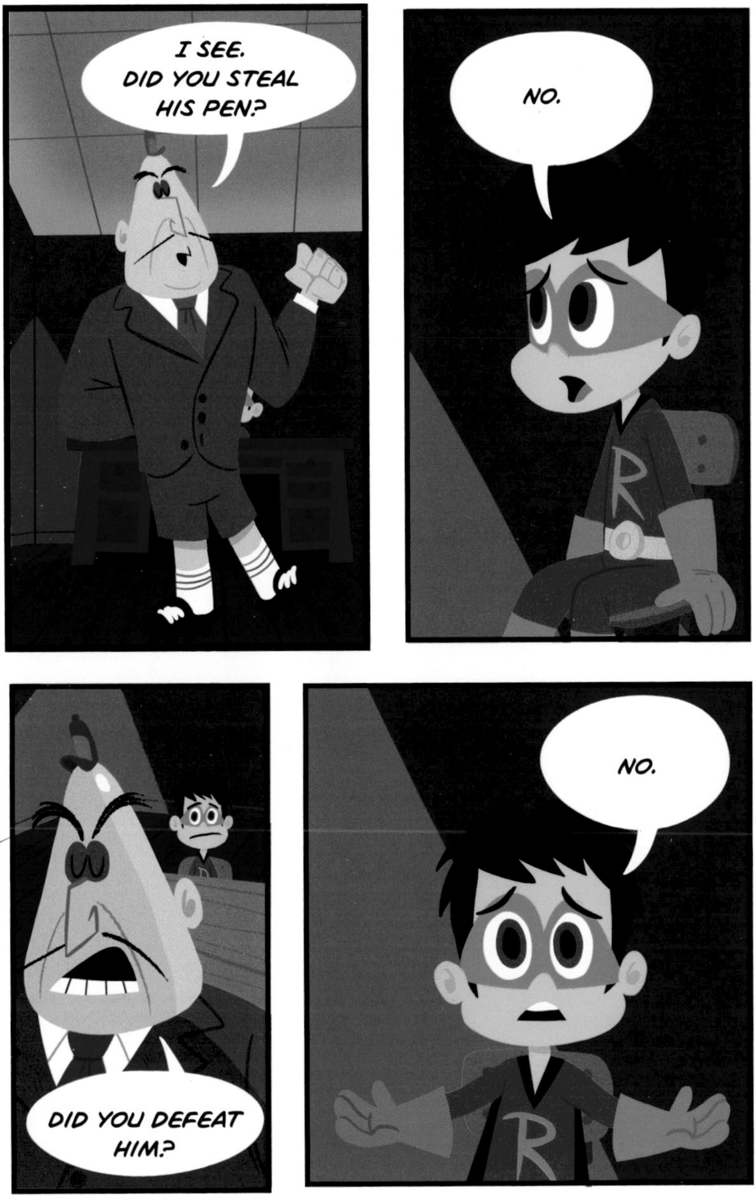
I SEE.
DID YOU STEAL HIS PEN?
NO.
DID YOU DEFEAT HIM?
NO.

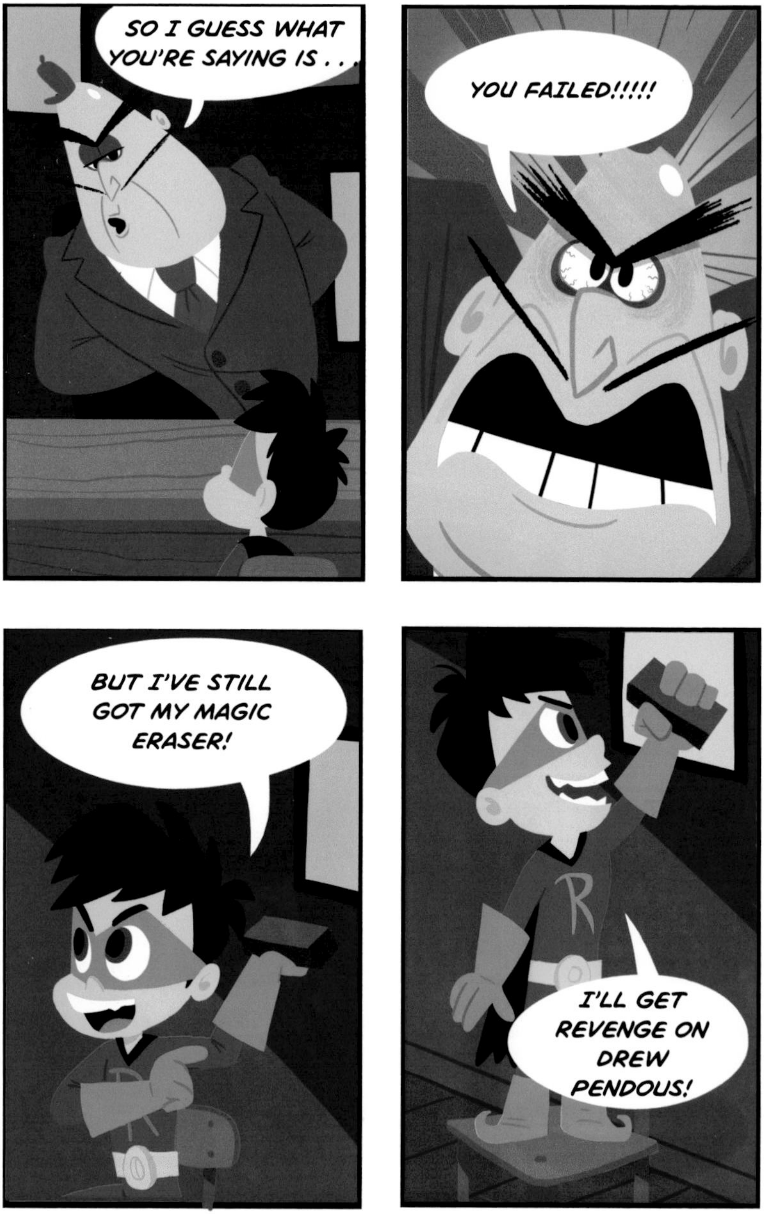
SO I GUESS WHAT YOU'RE SAYING IS . . .
YOU FAILED!!!!!
BUT I'VE STILL GOT MY MAGIC ERASER!
I'LL GET REVENGE ON DREW PENDOUS!

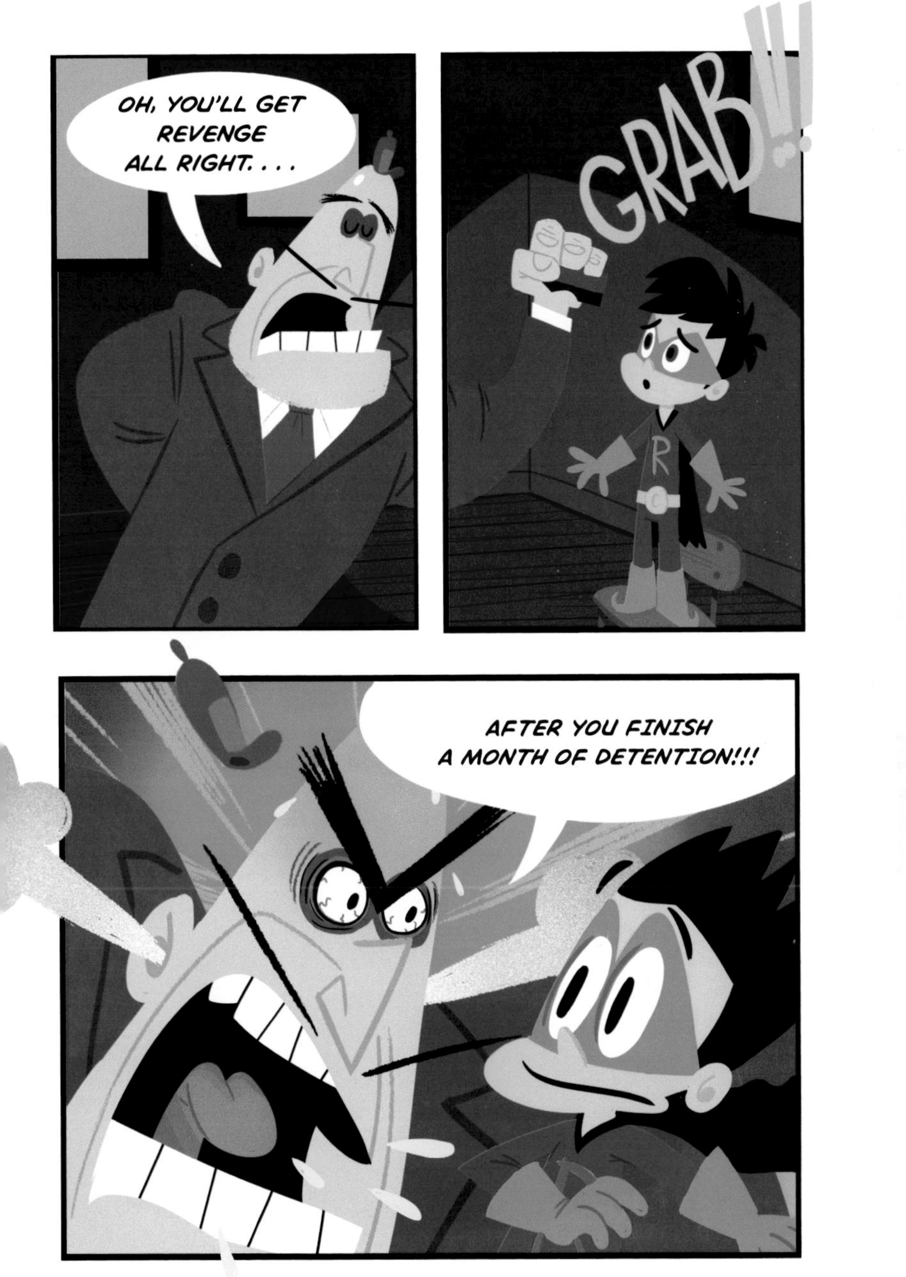
OH, YOU'LL GET REVENGE ALL RIGHT. . . .
GRAB!!!
AFTER YOU FINISH A MONTH OF DETENTION!!!

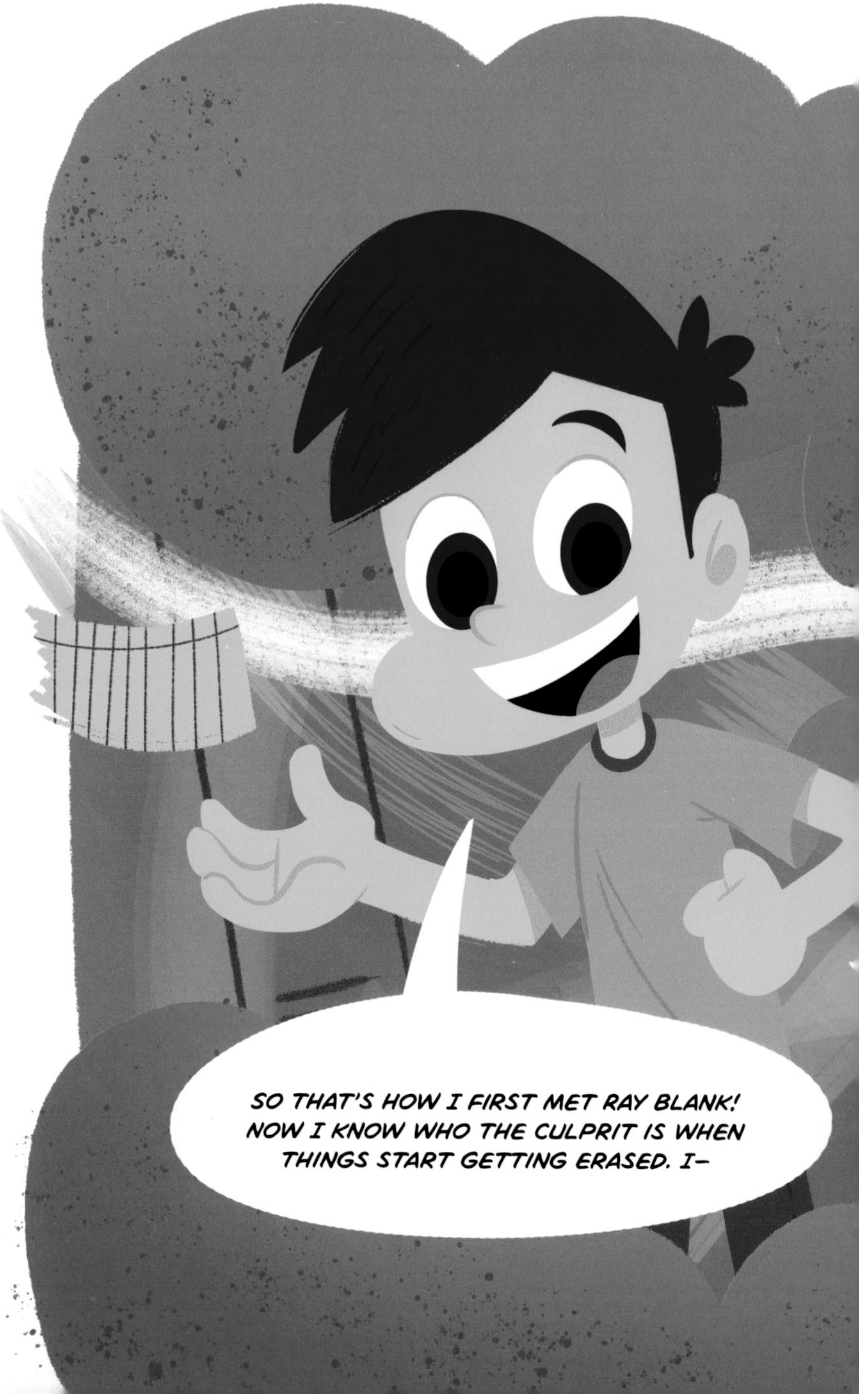
SO THAT'S HOW I FIRST MET RAY BLANK! NOW I KNOW WHO THE CULPRIT IS WHEN THINGS START GETTING ERASED. I–

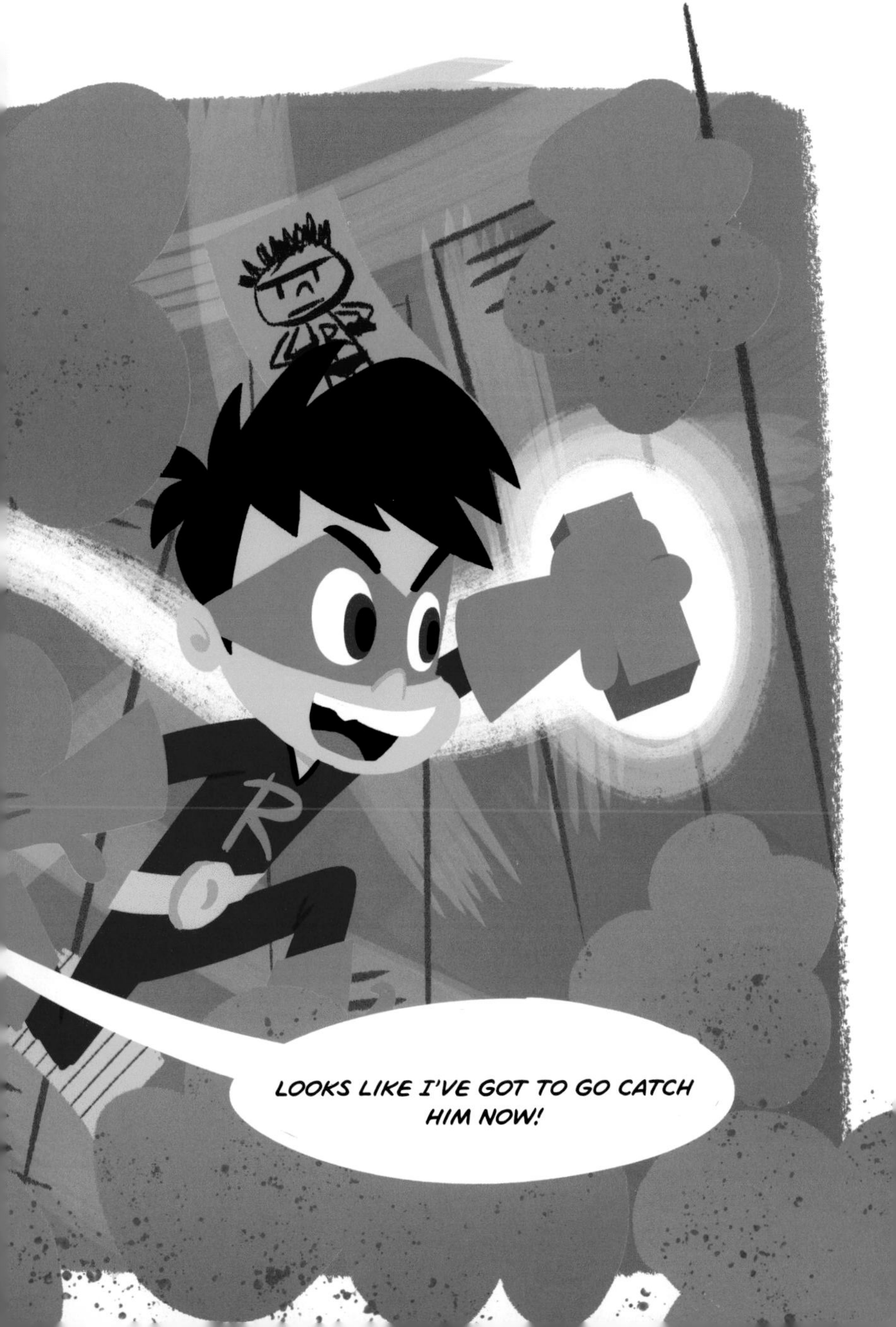
LOOKS LIKE I'VE GOT TO GO CATCH HIM NOW!